W9-BBX-470

CAMERON
AND THE GIRLS

by Edward Averett

CLARION BOOKS
Houghton Mifflin Harcourt
Boston • New York • 2013

Clarion Books

215 Park Avenue South

New York, New York 10003

Copyright © 2013 by Edward Averett

Clarion Books is an imprint of

Houghton Mifflin Harcourt Publishing Company.

www.hmhbooks.com

The text was set in 14-point Norlik.

Hand-lettering by Zachariah OHora

Library of Congress Cataloging-in-Publication Data

Averett, Edward, 1951–

Cameron and the girls / Edward Averett.

p. cm.

Summary: A boy suffering from schizophreniform disorder falls into a love triangle with
a girl in his junior high class—and a girl in his head.

ISBN 978-0-547-61215-7 (hardcover)

[1. Schizophrenia—Fiction. 2. Mental illness—Fiction. 3. Love—Fiction.] I. Title.

PZ7.A9345Cam 2013

[Fic]—dc23

2012015765

Manufactured in the United States of America

DOC 10 9 8 7 6 5 4 3 2 1

4500403270

For Penny. Miss you.

one

I'VE just walked the half mile down our driveway, and now I'm standing by the mailbox at our bus stop talking to myself. Which wouldn't be a bad thing, except that my sister, Beth, is standing with me.

"Stop doing that," she says.

"Stop doing what?"

"You know," she says. But I can tell she's mad about something else. "I hope Dad has a car wreck today," she adds. "He thinks he can actually ground me."

"Bad, huh?" I say.

"They're both going to be sorry one of these days," she says. Beth takes after our dad, who is a former semi-pro football player. She plays basketball and volleyball and towers over both me and our mom.

"Yeah," I say. "Sorry."

She smiles and adjusts her backpack. The sun is out now and the canvas starts smoking. "It's okay, Cam," she says. "I'm not going to do anything that'll get you in trouble."

"I know," I say. But there must be some kind of signal I give off because now Beth is suspicious. In the distance, we both hear the bus as its brakes squeal two stops away.

Beth tilts up my chin with her cold fingers and studies me like a bug in biology. "Are you doing what I think you're doing?" she says.

"Just one day," I say.

"Are you sure?"

"Well, maybe two."

"You forgot two days in a row?"

I shrug. The thing they all hate. "I didn't exactly forget."

Another squeal and the bus is one stop away.

"You okay?"

"Yeah. Why wouldn't I be?"

"Because if you're not taking your pills . . ." She fumbles for the words. "Don't you remember what happens?"

"It's an experiment," I say.

"Sure," she says. "I think Mom and Dad are a little tired of your experiments."

"It is," I insist. "It can be different this time. The doctor says it could just go away."

For a few seconds I can't tell if she's serious, but then she grins at me and rolls her eyes.

"Could be four or five or six days," I say.

Now Beth is stuck between laughter and worry. She just shakes her head as the bus comes around the corner. She jerks up her backpack. The bus squeaks to a stop and the doors bustle open. Before she boards, Beth turns and says, "Just don't make a fool out of the fam, okay?"

two

WE live on fifteen acres seven miles from town, and it's a long bus ride. There are a lot of kids to pick up in Lexington, Washington, but once we're through, the road curves alongside the river. I sit alone in my favorite window seat, staring out at the murky water. Up ahead, a railroad bridge crosses the river. As the road passes under it, I read a white sign with big red letters way up high:

DANGER! LOG TRAIN OVERHEAD!

It feels crowded, even though no one wants to sit in the seat with me. I hear Beth. Now that she's sixteen, she sits way in the back and talks to her friends. And then I hear another voice, and it makes me feel better. It's what I've been waiting for.

Here is what this voice is telling me:

```
It's eight thirty Pacific Standard Time.
What learning will we do today? Let's bring
that good brain of yours to full attention.
Intelligence is as intelligence does.
```

"Yes, sir," I say. And the kid sitting ahead of me turns and frowns.

I call the voice The Professor. His tone is so educated and knowledgeable. He talks to me with a kind of respect and appreciation for my gifts, not like to a kindergartner who can't understand basic English. The way my parents sometimes talk to me. Only Beth and The Professor treat me with respect. But now Beth has a boyfriend and a cell phone, so there's not much talking to her anymore.

There is a downside, as Dr. Simons would call it. In order to hear The Professor's voice, I have to stop taking my medication. I wasn't exactly lying to Beth. Today makes five days without it. There's good and there's bad with stopping. If it's mostly just hearing The Professor, then it's okay. But there can be other complications. Sometimes I'm not sure that what I actually hear and see is real. And then there can be problems, and, as Dr. Simons has told me, "Problems are like a match, and you shouldn't play with fire."

I've been in the hospital twice, both times since I was eleven years old.

Sometimes, the powers that be don't exactly know what they're dealing with, so they hedge their bets and don't make a definite diagnosis. "Rule out schizophreniform disorder" means it could be that disorder, but we don't have enough information to say for sure.

Even though that kind of disorder is not supposed to be very bad, it was very scary. For quite a while, I was feeling like somebody had taken over the controls in my brain. I told my mom that I wasn't feeling well, but in those days she paid more attention to physical problems, and she just put her hand on my forehead and told me I didn't have a fever.

I got weird. I liked staying in my room more. I hung by my knees from one of our apple trees for hours on end. It began to take a lot of effort just to say what my day was like when we were having dinner.

Then, one day, my brain split in two. As if the *Titanic* were leaving the dock in Liverpool and I was holding hands with my girlfriend and we didn't want to let go, and when we didn't, each hand broke off and the two hands went spinning down into the water. Obviously, I've never been to Liverpool and have never had a girlfriend, even though I would like one, so something was very wrong. I also heard voices, especially one that I didn't want to hear. He told me what to do and it wasn't always nice. I had to watch myself closely at that point.

I made such a bad scene once, I was put in the psych ward at the hospital. They shot me up with medications and made me take pills every day after that, and a year later I was doing pretty well, so they did a trial of no medications and everything was just fine. My parents thought it was the end of the story, but . . .

Something went wrong a few months ago.

"Diagnosis deferred" on your discharge papers generally means they can't figure out why it is happening again. They tell everyone that this new diagnosis is a step forward, that perhaps it will turn out that you have a lesser, more manageable illness.

My dad doesn't like things he doesn't understand. He said, "How can a kid the age of Cam be schizophrenic? He hasn't lived long enough to go crazy from life."

"It happens," said the doctor, shrugging. "And we're still quite hopeful that it isn't your classic schizophrenia."

"But what is it exactly?" asked my dad.

"Something different. Not quite so . . . ominous. If it's what we think it is, it can stay for a while, but never longer than six months. And fingers crossed, everybody, it can even disappear, never to return. There's no real predicting with this disease. Sometimes you just have to wait and see what happens."

"But Cameron is so young," my dad said, putting up the good-parent fight. "Isn't it more likely he's on drugs or something?"

The doc went on to explain that what I have is thought to have a genetic component. That set both my parents off as they searched their minds for the crazy ones in their families. One night I overheard them.

"Your aunt Agnes is a suspect," said my dad. "Remember how she used to hoard pennies in her shoes in the closet? Or your cousin Tootie. You remember all those jars of pee?"

But whenever I studied my mom she just looked plain scared as she chewed on her knuckles. Her face was always streaked red and her eyes leaked tears. As if she was only letting my dad go on and on about her family, to calm him down, to give him something to do.

But it was also as if she knew the reason I had this disease. My mom thinks it's her fault, that it's something she's done. And I think that's what makes her stalk me the way she does.

After a while, I see the school up ahead and start adjusting my backpack. As I do, I hear a voice I've never heard before.

Hello, Cam.

But there's no one next to me. I tap the kid in front on the shoulder. "Did you just say something?" I ask.

He shrugs my arm off his jacket. "Nutball," he says.

#

The bus stops and spits a lot of us out at my junior high school. Beth stays on until the high school, so when it starts to leave, I wave at her through the window. She smiles and gives me a cool wave.

Because I'm a two-time loser, I am now in the EDP, the Emotionally Disturbed Program, and we have our own special wing of the school that was added on when more and more kids started having emotional problems. The special wing keeps us from having to enter the school through the main doors, which can lead to trouble. One time, the little rabbit girl was grabbed and ended up hidden in a locker for most of the morning.

As I walk around to the side of the school, I wonder about the voice I heard on the bus. Sometimes it happens that way; a new voice doesn't stay too long, or it just turns out to be a real person talking to someone else. It's hard to know for sure. But this new voice. It was sweet. And soft. It was kind of a wow.

I bang on the narrow door at the back of the school. In a minute, Mrs. Owens, my teacher, pushes it open.

"Well, hello there, Cameron," she says.

I breeze past her and smell the perfume drifting from her loose clothes. Mrs. Owens has been on a diet for most of the school year and now her clothes just hang off her.

"You look skinny today," I tell her, and she pats me on the back as she pulls the door closed.

"You little sweet talker," she says. I know I'm one of her favorites because a lot of kids in our class are troublemakers. Most of them can't sit still. It seems like Mrs. Owens spends most of her time sorting out everybody's symptoms instead of teaching. One time, I found her in the supply closet, sitting on a bucket and crying.

Today, I find my seat next to Griffin. Griffin likes to puff out his cheeks and then squirt air past his gums so as to make rude noises. The trouble with Griffin is that he is too smart. He learned so much so fast that his brain couldn't keep up. Now information falls out of it as fast as Griffin can take it in.

"So here we are again, big boy," he says, studying a greasy clump of dark hair that tries to cover his eye.

"Yeah," I say. "Again."

When we get settled, Mrs. Owens takes the roll call. She comes to my name and looks up. "Cameron, I got a note from the librarian. You've a book overdue."

At that, Griffin shoots up his hand. "Cameron wants to know if we get any extra time in the library this week."

"I do not," I say.

"It depends," says Mrs. Owens, checking over the roll sheet. "You need to be better focused for that to happen."

The other trouble with Griffin is that I can never tell him anything, not even about the library. "I can talk for myself," I whisper.

I try to glare at Griffin, but he just smiles big and says, "Right."

After she's finished with the roll call, Mrs. Owens walks up to the chalkboard and picks up a piece of colored chalk. She trades it from one hand to the other as she says, "Today I have chosen a very, very interesting topic for us to discuss."

While I would like to listen to her soothing voice, another, more soothing one steals into my brain.

Even if you know the instructor is not

doing her best work, as her student you must act as if you're learning everything she has to offer. This is essential for one's future. Know what your goal is. Cream rises to the top.

It could become a battle now. I have to pay attention to keep Mrs. Owens in focus at the front of the classroom while The Professor serves up some more interesting conversation in my mind. It's a battle I've waged before. I'm determined to win it this time, but winning it can be tricky.

three

TODAY, it's harder for me to wake up. And when I do, it's harder to tell the difference between waking and sleeping. But because I've stopped taking my pills, I have to be as normal as I can be, or somebody's going to notice.

I jump out of bed and run to the bathroom at the end of the hall. The door is shut and I can hear water running. I hop from one foot to the other, finally pound on the door.

"In a minute," Beth says.

But Beth's minutes last longer than anyone else's, and so I have to sprint down the stairs to the bathroom next to my parents' bedroom. Normally, after I go, I sneak back up the stairs and get ready. But this morning, as I reach to flush the toilet, something sweet and unexpected interrupts my routine.

Hello, Cam.

I freeze. There it is again. Clearer this time. It's got a higher pitch than what I'm used to, and the words kind of take their time getting said. And hearing those words is like licking syrup.

"What?" I say. But I get nothing in return. Instead, The Professor cranks up:

```
In difficult situations, it serves one
best to keep one's voice down.
```

And he's right. "Cameron?" It's my mom outside the bathroom door. I check the mirror: sleepy-looking hair, a little red in my eyes, pale face.

"Good," I say, and then open the door and step out. Mom stands in her turquoise robe and studies me.

"It's okay," I say. "Really."

Before I can walk away, she grabs me by the arm and turns me toward her. She puts her microscope eyes on and makes me squirm.

"Did you take them?" she finally says.

I hate to lie, especially to her. I lick my lips and feel a chill wind on my bare legs. "Course I did," I say. She lets me go.

Beth and I have to jog to get to the bus on time. In

my seat, I try to figure out the other voice. It sounded like a girl, which is unusual because I have never heard from a girl in my life. Maybe it's just a boy with a high voice. No, definitely a girl. Maybe it's someone trying to fool me. There are always other kids out there trying to make a fool of me. It's better not to tell anyone about this in case it's true. But it was definitely a girl.

#

I didn't take my medication again. The previous record was eight straight days before anything happened. Now this is the sixth. I have to do my regular head check. There is a slight buzz in the back of my brain, but it's not bad yet. I can still think over the top of it. I hold my hands out straight in front of me. No tremors, at least none that will attract attention. That's good. I can handle this kind of normal me.

But my mom can be the best detective. Stopping my meds is her worst nightmare because she thinks they're the magic glue that will hold us all together. If she suspects anything at all, she'll go snooping around, and if she finds anything suspicious, then I'm in for it. We'll have that fight we always have where she asks me why I do things like that and I have to answer that I can't help it. But she doesn't accept that answer, and I will have to end up saying, "I hate my life." Which is true most of the time.

"You don't hate your life," my mom will struggle to say. "You just think you do."

"Well, what's reality, then? Is it what I think or what other people think?"

"Talk normally, Cameron," she will say quietly. "Please."

But I don't feel like fighting anymore. I don't feel like explaining myself anymore. Is this too much to wish for?

If I take the meds, my life is lonely and awkward and hopeless and other kids are mean to me. But if I don't take them, I get The Professor and now this girl and who knows what other fun and interesting things. It's my own life I have to live. Don't I get to choose?

#

At school, I pound and pound on the back door, but Mrs. Owens doesn't come. All around me, kids are hurrying to get to class on time. I start to feel nervous. I run around toward the front, my backpack thumping against my butt.

I climb the wide concrete steps, arranged in half-moons all the way up. I open one of the big glass and metal doors, and the warm air, full of sweat and testosterone and floor wax, rushes to greet me.

I stand and get my bearings. I can't seem to remember how to get to Mrs. Owens's room from here. Kids bump into me and cuss me out as they pass. Down one hallway is a sea of bobbing heads. Down the other way, the same.

Two girls dressed all in black approach me. I try to look away, but they're like rattlesnakes and I'm their kangaroo rat. They walk around my body, checking me up and down. Even their lipstick is black.

"You new?" they ask in unison.

"I don't know the way," I blurt out. Girls make me feel like crying and touching myself at the same time. My heart beats like a wild snare drum.

"Oh baby," one of the girls says, drawing close. She takes me by the collar of my shirt and pulls me tight into her face. I can smell her smoky breath. "Do I turn you on?" she asks.

In a way, she does, but I say no quickly and watch her smile go south, her cheeks tighten. A devilish sneer takes shape on her black lips.

"Hey, you're a nut boy, aren't you?" she says.

Before I can answer, she shoves me backwards, and the momentum drives me into two other kids, who in turn shove me away. I bounce like a pinball for a while until I slam against the hard tiled wall.

From there I watch the kids thin out. Then the bell

rings and only hollow footsteps echo down the hall. Now I can't quite keep the tears away, and I feel those traitors pooling in my eyes. I mourn in the hallway, remembering how open and fun life was before I was old enough for school. How I could run fast and jump high and everybody clapped.

Soon, Mrs. Johnson, the school secretary, sticks her head out of the office. She spies me and hurries over.

"What's the matter, Cam?" she asks.

But I can only shake my head. The words lodge in my throat, and besides, they aren't the kind of words Mrs. Johnson is looking for.

"I can't find my room," I finally manage to stutter.

"Ah, boy-o," she says, taking me by the arm. "I've had days like that."

As I follow her down the hall, The Professor says:

With such a minor injury from that last shove, the head generally stops throbbing in a few minutes. Shirts should be tucked in. Zippers zipped. All prepared for class. It's been said that schizophreniform disorder differs from other schizophrenic disorders in the length and severity of the episodes. It can begin at a very young age and end abruptly, never to return, before adulthood.

In spite of the hopeful news from The Professor, I have just about come to the conclusion that adulthood is a long way away and I may never be able to mingle again with normal kids.

#

Mrs. Owens is sick and we have a substitute teacher, Mr. Frye. He is tall and clean, wears a dark blue suit. On his face, a short goatee fences his mouth. When Mrs. Johnson brings me in, Mr. Frye is standing at the front of the class with his arms folded. In one of his hands he carries a stopwatch and he glances at it from time to time. The room is deathly quiet. I can see that Griffin's face is red and he holds one of his legs still while the other bounces up and down. The captive leg is like a hobbled pony just dying to rear back and kick out.

Mrs. Johnson says, "I found this one — "

But Mr. Frye puts up his hand to stop her. He says, "Five, four, three, two, one." All around the room, the students let out their breath. Griffin's leg bounces high and hits the underside of his desk. Slowly, Mr. Frye turns toward Mrs. Johnson. "Now, what were you saying?"

Mrs. Johnson harrumphs and places me in front of her. "One of yours," she says, then turns tail and leaves the room.

"Another one?" he says. "Well, find your seat and let's get going. You won't have the benefit of our breathing and quiet exercise because you're late, but see to it that you don't get disruptive."

Mr. Frye gives us a reading assignment and then sits down at the desk. There are four manila folders in front of him, and he picks one up, pulls out a few pages, and starts to read. Every once in a while, he shoots his head up and looks intently at a student. One time, he looks at me.

He closes the folder and gets up, walking slowly around the room. He dawdles behind kids who act as if they are reading the assignment. He finally stops behind me and then drops to his haunches. "Just so you know," he whispers, leaning in. "My brother had what you have as a kid, and now it's smooth sailing for him. Owns his own house. Has a boat. Two kids."

I wonder why strangers do that with me. Like receptionists at the doctor's office. Clerks at the Safeway. As if I'm in a minority group that everybody's dying to identify with.

"I don't want to talk about it," I whisper.

Mr. Frye nods and stands up. He starts to walk off and I think I'm home free.

But not yet. "Well, if you ever want to, you could talk to me."

I don't like this stranger so close and ask if I can use the bathroom. Once there, I look in the big mirror and watch myself take long, easy breaths. "There must be a reason for all this," I say. I splash water on my face and then collect some in my two cupped palms. It shimmers in the light. From the side, I think I can see an image, a picture of somebody, but I'm not sure. I tilt my head as I hear the door open behind me. The picture in the water is a girl. From behind, I hear a girl's voice.

"What are you doing in here?"

I whirl around, and there is a girl I recognize from the regular classes.

"You retard," she says. "Get out before I call somebody."

I realize I'm in the girls' bathroom. The shame runs up my windpipe. "Sorry," I mumble, and I run around her and out into the hall.

I want to go home, but it is only the start of the school day, and if I do, my parents will wonder why. The school will wonder why. There will be questions that I can't answer. Better to pull myself together and act as if everything is just fine. That's what they want, after all. That everything be just fine.

Fine. Fine. Fine. Fine. Fine.

#

I last the day with no more stupid mistakes. Mr. Frye can't really give us new lessons, so there is a lot of reading to do. I'm a pretty good reader. As a matter of fact, I'm good at most things. Except for team sports and anything that has to do with a partner. I generally get a three in "Works Well with Others." A three means I don't get along very well at all.

I run from the bus stop, ignoring Beth and the drizzle. I know the way so well that I can turn my face up to the sky and feel what probably no one else can feel: the clouds shining down on me. Dr. Simons once said that everyone else should be so lucky to see the things that only I can see.

But I hate that the substitute talked to me, and thinking that makes the cloud shine go away. If people say your life is confidential, then it should be confidential. But how can it be if any old substitute can come in and read about me from a big manila envelope? It's not fair because I don't even get a chance to prove myself, and I'm sure I look way too crazy on paper.

But things are changing. I can feel something good creeping up.

"Wish me luck," I whisper to no one in particular.

Good luck, I hear.

"Thanks," I say.

And people say I don't communicate well.

four

I WAKE up warm because the vent in the wall in my room is throwing out heat in waves. It is still dark and I can hear soft rain against the window. I would like to snuggle down and go back to sleep, but I feel tense. I stretch the muscles in my back and legs until they hurt. Physical pain sometimes postpones the mental.

But one thing I have learned is that the mental always comes. First, there is a stab somewhere in my mind, as if somebody were slitting my thinking with a sharp knife. With my eyes closed, I can actually visualize words bisecting and falling away. The *good-* says goodbye to the *-ness*. But it's hard to tolerate this progression of weirdness for very long, so I slide out of bed and get dressed.

There are secret ways to get out of the house without my parents' knowledge. The best one is in the living room near the fireplace. It's a built-in wood box that connects through the wall to the wide front porch. On the other side is a box that looks the same. Someone on the porch can throw fireplace logs into the box, and they will roll inside, where someone else can lift them out and throw them on the fire.

Since it's late in the season, the wood box is nearly empty. I squeeze down into this coffin and then wriggle across to the other side. Like a vampire, I crawl out and stand shivering on the porch. It is dark all around except for the headlights of a lone car way down on the highway near the bus stop. I love this time all by myself. No one to watch me shake the way I am shaking now. The tension pushes me off the porch. I stand on the grass. The rain is coming down even harder and I soak it up.

Behind me, the ghostly light of day is starting to creep over the hills, but it is still too dark to see well. I turn around and around, making myself dizzy. On about my tenth turn, I hear this:

Hello, Cam.

I turn my head sharply; my heartbeat picks up.

"Who?" I whisper hoarsely.

It's me.

"But who are you?"

I hear a faint giggle.

You are so funny. You know who I am.

"I'm funny?" I don't even feel the rain now, even though it has soaked through me.

It's one of the things I like about you.

"You like me?" I say. No girl, except for Beth, has ever said anything like that. I am tingling now.

Of course I do.

I stick out my tongue and lap at the raindrops like a dog at a water bowl. "What else do you like about me?" I ask.

Well, I like that you're a thinker. That you're not always out throwing baseballs or footballs or spitting on the sidewalk.

"Sometimes I like to throw a football," I say.

But it's not your whole life, Cameron. You're more than just that one thing. You speak like a much older person. You read up on interesting subjects, like psychology. In fact, you're sort of like a Renaissance man.

This could possibly be the best moment of my entire life, but the front porch light suddenly snaps on and the door is yanked open. My mom is standing there cinching her robe.

"I'm not doing anything," I quickly say.

She stands quietly, looking old and tired in this moment of silence. I do that to people. If I laid out all the moments of silence I have created for others in my life, they would make a whole long quiet life of their own.

My mom finally says, "This can't be happening again."

I walk up to the porch and stand in front of her. I've let her down one more time; I can see it in her eyes. It's not what I want to do.

"I'm sorry, Mom," I say.

She steps aside. "Go in and change out of those."

"Okay," I say in my obedient voice.

But as I pass her, she adds, "We're going to have to talk about this, Cam."

Back in my room, I tear off my clothes, dry myself, and slip down under the covers. I shiver until I hear her mount the stairs. Soon, I can feel her in the doorway. I project out my force field to keep her from saying anything or getting too close. She sighs as she picks up my sloppy wet clothes. Maybe there are some things she doesn't want to know for sure because she doesn't come in any farther.

When she's gone, my mind considers what's just happened. With voices, it's a crapshoot. You can't always control what you get. But I've never felt this way from just hearing one of them. As if my blood were juicier than normal. I don't know what her name is, but I think I'll call her The Girl.

In spite of the warm air spilling out of the vent, I'm too psyched to fall back to sleep, and I eventually get up to get ready for school.

five

AT school, there are only two girls in my class. Amy, the little rabbit girl, is always showing her big front teeth as she chatters away. The other one is named Nina. She came a couple of weeks ago and usually keeps to herself. I like her anyway. It's easier to make up stories about girls who keep to themselves, because they don't give themselves away. She has great hair, which is rich and dark and long. It cascades in waves from the top of her head. And she is always swinging it back and forth. Especially when she doesn't know the answer to a question.

I'm not sure what her problem is, but I know she must have one, otherwise she wouldn't be in the EDP. Today I sit in my seat and watch her hair. It moves in a fancy rhythm that makes me think of things better kept inside my head.

Soon she turns and catches me staring at her. My eyes dart to the front of the class, and I pretend I wasn't looking. But I can't help myself and snatch another glance. She's still looking. I try to smile, but the tension in my face won't let me. She shrugs and turns back.

From the front of the class, Mrs. Owens is saying, "If the South had won the Civil War, what do you think the United States would be like today?" She stops and picks up a hanky to wipe her very red nose.

Griffin quickly shoots up his hand. "It would be like no North."

"What do you mean?" Mrs. Owens asks.

"Well, I mean it would be all South. There would be, you know, no direction called north. The country would be called the United Southern States of America."

At first I think Nina is whispering to me, and I turn her way. But she is tracing the picture of George Washington on the front of her history book.

Still, there is a voice.

Cam?

It's The Girl's voice again, soft and sweet. "I'm here," I stutter in a whisper, which unfortunately draws Griffin's attention. He elbows me.

"Good," says Mrs. Owens, talking about Griffin's answer.

Don't you want to talk to me, Cam?

"I do," I say. "I do want to talk to you."

Griffin elbows me again and it hurts this time. I rub at it, trying to frown him away.

"Does anyone have an idea of what the United States would look like if the South had won the war?" pleads Mrs. Owens.

But no one does, and when class is over, we file down to the cafeteria. I can smell the fish sticks before I go through the door. Someone taps me on the shoulder, and I turn to see Nina right behind me.

"Why were you staring at me?" she asks.

"I wasn't staring at you," I say. I want to keep my brain fresh and open for the new voice, and talk is distracting. The crowd of kids pushes us farther into the cafeteria. We bump close, and I feel a tingling in the spot where we touch.

"You were," she says. "I saw you."

Griffin wags his tongue at her. "He wants you, that's why," he says.

"You're disgusting," says Nina. She looks at me. "I mean him, not you." Then she hurries to catch up to the line forming by the trays.

After I get my plate, I sit down and roll up one sleeve

to look at the spot where Griffin elbowed me. It's made a bright red ring. I rub at it and look around. Nina is sitting by herself. But she disappears when Griffin stands in the way making faces while he balances his tray. I try to laugh but can't.

Cam, I want you to know that I'm here just for you. I think you're a great guy.

"But who are you?" I whisper.

I'm whoever you want me to be. I'm your girlfriend.

And there is a peace to what she says. I feel calmer immediately. Giddy calm. When Griffin finally sits down, I inch away from him.

"Who're you talking to, man?" he asks.

"I don't want to talk right now," I say. I know it's not good to say that, and I know that keeping to myself is one of my symptoms, but sometimes I just can't stand communicating with anybody. And Griffin has a problem with keeping his mouth shut.

#

After school, on the bus, I'm sitting by myself again, but I'm not feeling all that alone now. Maybe it's the new voice. I jump when Beth taps me on the shoulder.

"Cameron? What are you doing?"

"Nothing," I say.

"Your lips were moving. Who were you talking to?"

"Nobody. Please shut up."

But Beth is not satisfied. She kneels beside me. "You'd better start taking those pills again," she says. She pets my head, but I knock her hand away.

"Mom's going to be looking for you," she says.

"Can't you all just leave me alone?"

"Do you want to hear what Mom asked me or not?"

I consider this for a moment and then nod.

"Good," she says. "She thinks you're not taking your medication."

"Good for her."

"Don't worry," says Beth, digging into her pocket. She pulls out my meds and holds the little plastic bottle between her thumb and forefinger. "She was looking for it, but I found it before she did." She tosses it to me. "You might want to hide a few of those before she gets hold of it."

I jam the bottle in my pocket and then take a peek at Beth. "Thanks," I say.

"You know you could take those once in a while and still conduct your little scientific — whatever — experiment."

"You don't understand."

Beth scrunches up her lips and then raises her eyebrows. "Listen, Cam, you were mumbling to nobody just then. Remember what I said about embarrassing the family?" She stands up and heads back toward her seat, but I yell after her.

"You haven't been talking to me today, have you, Sis?"

She stops and studies me again. "What do you mean?"

"Maybe through telepathy or ESP or something."

"Geez," she says, looking around at the kids who heard me ask it. She puts a finger to her lips and shakes her head before finding her seat.

"Well?"

But the conversation is over for her. I have to learn not to push people too far.

six

I PUT a bunch of pills in my pocket and sneak the bottle back into the upstairs bathroom. And just in time, too, because before it's lights out, Mom comes up and starts rummaging in there. As I slip into bed, I can hear her popping the top off the bottle and shaking it. In another minute she's in my room.

She plants her hand on my forehead and keeps it there. "We should talk about this morning," she says.

"It's nothing," I say.

"Cam," she says evenly. "You could have caught pneumonia out there like that."

I try to change the subject. "School's hard," I say. "Mrs. Owens asks hard questions."

But she shakes her head. "No, it's more than that. I've seen it before. You were talking."

This is not good. I know that when she starts to ask questions, pretty soon they will all pile up, and before you know it, I'll have an appointment at the doctor.

"Cameron. Please tell me. It sounded like you were maybe talking back to a voice."

I sit up in my bed. "Mom."

"I know it makes you mad. But what I saw. What I heard. It makes me think . . ."

I pull my arms out from under the blanket and rest them on the fuzzy top. I take a deep breath and try to clear my brain. It whirls a little, but I still have control. "I have a girlfriend," I say boldly.

Mom blinks and jerks back as if she's been hit. "No, really, Cam," she says.

"Really."

"You have a girlfriend?"

"I was practicing talking to her last night."

She sits down on the edge of my bed. I can tell she wants so much to believe me.

"Is it not okay?" I say.

"No, it's not that, it's just that it's so surprising."

"Not to me."

She places a warm hand on mine. "That's wonderful,

Cam. Just wonderful." She pauses and then says, "Is it someone I know?"

I shake my head. "I don't think so. She's new."

"A new girl," she says with wonderment. "I see."

I hope she won't ask more specific questions, and I'm relieved when she stands up again. "Well, that explains a lot." She kisses me and on her way to the door, stops. "I have a confession to make, Cam. I thought maybe you had stopped taking your meds."

"Mom."

"I know, I know. But I'm glad you haven't stopped, and I'm glad you have a girlfriend. But maybe next time you can practice talking to her indoors."

I hear her cross the hall and say good night to Beth by patting the door a couple of times. I'm not certain she's convinced, but I'm happy she's gone because I need to stretch out my legs and keep them stiff for a while. They creak and pop. My stomach is flip-flopping; I have a headache. I fear I will start to break, but:

Hello, Cam. How's my man today?

It's as if she's been hiding under my bed, waiting for Mom to leave. "Better now," I say. Her voice once again wraps me in a warm cottony cloud. I wish I could feel her next to me. "Tell me what you look like," I quickly say.

Why don't you guess?

I close my eyes and try to picture her. A blurry image appears, and I try to bring it into focus. "Short brown hair."

Good.

"Brown eyes. Red lips. Top one thinner than the bottom one. A smile that makes the sun shine."

Oh, a poet.

I squirm a little. "Soft delicate fingers like your voice. And smart. Your face looks smart."

How did you know?

I shrug.

Anything else?

I don't have to think long. "And curvy," I say. "Your body is curvy."

Thank you, Cam. That's sweet. And guess what? You're absolutely right about everything.

I can sense my blood pumping all over again. It makes me feel alive.

"Thank you," I say.

For what?

"Just for being here with me. That's all."

You're entirely welcome, Cam. I feel love when we're together. I like that.

Her voice is so lush, so nectarish, that I let myself taste it. I sense a strong familiar pulse in my body that feels good. I can go on listening to her forever. And realizing that that's exactly what I want to do, I snuggle down deep in the warm blanket. I let her voice envelop me.

#

Dad's not up yet, so it is just Mom, Beth, and me at the table. Beth and my mom are having another fight. Beth accuses her of being too much of a tyrant and compares our home to Nazi Germany. And that always gets my mother's dander up.

"There is no way on God's green earth that this house is like the Nazis," she insists. "And I am very offended that you would even say that."

"Be offended all you want, Mom," says Beth. "I'm sixteen and I should have rights."

Mom stretches her hand out, palm up. "I'm going to have to ask for your cell," she says.

Beth shakes her head and looks like lightning has hit her.

"Now, Beth!" Mom's voice echoes in my head.

Slowly, Beth reaches into her purse and pulls out her bright-pink phone. She stares at it a moment and then tosses it on the table.

Nothing is resolved, and Beth leaves the house in such a huff that I have to run to catch up with her. "Leave me alone," she says before I can open my mouth. She swings her backpack around so violently that I think she'll slam it into me.

She takes off again. We are getting closer to the tangle of evergreen blackberry vines that hide the side road from the driveway.

"For your information," she says, "Mom will now spend the rest of the day feeling all guilty because she took my phone, and by the time I get home, she'll want to apologize and let me do whatever I want."

"Like what?" I say.

"Like this." On the other side of the blackberries a maroon Honda sits idling.

"Who's that?" I say.

As if to answer, a boy I recognize but don't know steps out of the car. He is all grin, with long dark blond hair falling in thin strands on his forehead. "Hey cutes," he says.

Beth runs up and kisses him on the lips. I have never seen her do this with anyone before, and I feel embarrassed. She turns back and says, "If you tell a soul, your ass is dead."

"Don't worry," I say.

"Meet Dylan," she says.

My brain backs up a step. I feel a wobble in the air. Dylan gives me a little wave and I squeak out, "Hey."

"You want a ride to school?" Beth asks.

"In that?" I say, pointing to the car.

"What did you think?"

I'm not sure I like this new sister of mine. She seems to be putting on a show. But I don't want to ride the bus alone, and I agree to go with them.

They put me in the back next to schoolbooks, backpacks, and a floor full of dirty wrappers. The car smells like the outside of McDonald's.

"Now, drive carefully," says Beth, "so you don't attract attention."

But Dylan doesn't care about attention and pulls out fast, throwing gravel all over the berry bushes. Beth slugs him but she laughs and moves closer.

It is a different scene I see out the window, closer to the ground, as we motor through Lexington and along the West Side Highway. I can barely see the river over the top of the dike. Beth and Dylan are talking low in the front seat, and every once in a while, Beth laughs. It is a good laugh and reminds me of The Girl's voice.

Unlike all the good feelings I had last night, something is wrong in my head this morning. It feels a little growly and dark. I have to fight to make my thoughts straight. Something inside me is waking up and flexing its muscles. It feels like I'm falling over, even though

I'm sitting up straight. Behind my eyelids, bright yellow flashes get in the way, and when I open my eyes, no matter how hard I try to avoid those lights, they follow me.

But the worst part is the low rumble I hear at the back of my head. Like distant thunder before a whopper of a storm. I sit nervously in the seat and rub my arms.

Beth glances back and frowns. "You okay?" she says.

"What's the forecast?" I say.

This makes Dylan laugh, but Beth narrows her eyes. "Be careful," she finally says. "I heard you in your room with Mom last night."

"What did you hear?" I ask.

"I heard you talking about a girlfriend."

"Girlfriend?" says Dylan. "The little guy has a girlfriend?"

"I'm not little," I say.

Beth gives me her warning look and sits back straighter. "Maybe," says Beth. Then she leans in to Dylan again and kisses him on the cheek.

"Yowzer," says Dylan as he caresses her chin.

Seeing them like this, I can feel it in every part of me. I want what they have.

seven

THE next day is Friday and a lot of kids are sick, including the gym teacher, Mr. Fundseth. The substitute has the class go on a walk for exercise. I'm the last one out, and I'm already way behind the others. I start to jog, but I hear a voice.

"Hey." The voice comes from my left, between the shop and mechanical-drawing buildings; Nina is leaning with her hands flat against a wall. "Wait up," she says. She walks over. "I thought you'd never come out."

"I don't really want to," I say.

She studies my face. "Are you okay?"

"Yes, are you?"

She shrugs. "Not really, but what else is new?"

I look over to the walkers, who are quite far away.

"You don't really want to go with them," she says.

"Not really."

"That's the right answer," she says as she takes hold of my shirt. "Come on with me."

We're walking in the lot and I look around. The class is almost out of sight now. Cars are speeding by in front of the school. One small red one revs its engine before it shoots across the street into the lot. At the same time, I realize Nina has stopped.

"Oh, great," she says. I turn and see a ghostly look on her face.

The engine revs again and a horn honks. Now the red car is very close to us. I notice paint on the windows and tin cans tied to the back bumper. The driver's window glides down, and a woman with uncombed frosty hair pokes her head out. A cigarette juts from her mouth. "Hey, baby girl," she says.

"Go away," Nina says.

"Got a live one," the woman says, laughing. There is a skinny unshaven man in the passenger seat, and he laughs too.

I look at the writing on the back window. Just Married, it says.

"Listen, I'm going to be away for a couple," the woman says. "Think you can take care of things while I'm gone?"

"Just go," Nina says.

"That's the sport," the woman says. "There's some money on the table to tide you over." She puts the car in gear, revs the engine one more time, and peels out, the cans clanking behind her.

Nina and I watch her go. "Who's that?" I say, but I know.

"My so-called mother," she says.

"Did she just get married?"

Nina looks at me as if I have no brain. "She just does stuff like that to get attention. She's still married to some other guy. She thinks she's so cute."

Nina's mom has rounded the corner now and passes the last of the walkers. The substitute is no longer craning his neck to check for stragglers.

Nina takes me by the arm again. "Come on, let's go."

I let her drag me along. "Where are we going?"

"I want something to eat," she says. "And ever since they took the candy machines out, there's nowhere to get it except at the gas mart."

The gas mart sits a couple of blocks away. "But we're not supposed to leave the school grounds."

"Yeah? So?"

"So we can't go to the store."

Nina makes a big deal of putting her hands on her

hips. "Look around. Do you see anybody stopping us?"

I do look around again. The lot is empty. I suddenly feel a pain in my chest and rub at it. The thunder in the back of my brain has not left since it started yesterday. I can feel Nina studying me again, and I visualize myself behind thick glass at the zoo.

"Well?" She taps her foot on the asphalt.

I open my mouth, but before I can speak:

`One should try to be law-abiding.`

Saved by The Professor. "I prefer to be law-abiding," I say.

`There are always better things for young minds to do.`

"There are better things for young minds . . ." I stop and consider what I'm saying. "We could get detention."

Nina shakes her head. "Cameron, we're already in the EDP. Is that the worst thing you can think of?" She takes off for the street.

I hurry to catch up and am nearly clipped by a car as I sprint across.

"Why are you in there, anyway?" I ask. "You seem pretty normal."

"I am normal," she says, not looking at me. "It's everybody else who's nuts." She takes a few more steps and adds, looking at the ground, "I'm, you know, depressed."

"Oh," I say. "Is it bad?"

"You ever been depressed? If you have, then you wouldn't ask that stupid question."

"Sorry," I say.

"Don't worry about it."

"You talk a lot," I say. "I mean, in class you're so quiet."

"That's because I've got nothing to say to those other nuts."

I wish we could slow down, but Nina seems bent on a mission. We cover the block or so to the store in record time. In front of it, a man with a full bright-red beard is filling his SUV with gas.

"I live down there in that house," Nina says, pointing.

I follow her finger about halfway down the block and see a small, boxy red house. The grass is already high in the yard, and old pruned rhododendron branches are strewn all around. "Nice," I say.

When I look back, Nina is holding out her hand. "You got any change?"

"No."

"Hmm. How are we going to get any candy?"

I have no answer, but something odd begins to happen. Her face is changing before my eyes. I shake my head, but it still happens. Her mouth turns down, her cheeks wrinkle up, and suddenly her eyes are full of tears. I think maybe I'm hallucinating.

I start to say, "I'd better . . ."

But Nina walks over toward the island where the bearded man is topping off his tank. She starts talking to him, barely loud enough for me to hear. I can see her back shake, her hand come up to her face and cover her eyes. Then, like a miracle, the man reaches in his pocket and pulls out a pile of change. Nina picks and chooses from the pile and comes back.

"Nice guy," she says, passing me and going inside.

I am relieved I wasn't hallucinating after all and watch her through the glass. Her face is back to normal again as she checks out the candy aisle.

In a minute, she comes back out with red licorice and a Snickers bar. She hands me one of the licorice pieces.

"There now, that wasn't difficult, was it?"

I've never hung around with anyone like her before. Although I am still worried about being away from school, I also feel sort of adventurous. I jam the licorice in my mouth and chew hard.

"What are you in the class for?" she asks. "Besides just being weird."

"I don't work well with others."

"What's that mean?"

"It means in the normal classes I get a little hard to handle."

"Do you have ADD?"

"No."

"What, then?"

"Schizo."

She doesn't flinch the way most people do. "You got a shrink?"

I tell her about Dr. Simons and the tufts of hair on his knuckles, his tall cupboard full of med samples.

We start walking in unison back down the street. I wonder how we do that when neither one of us has said anything about it.

"I take Zoloft," Nina says. "It's an antidepressant, but it makes me suicidal."

Suicidal is a word that I stay away from. It's a word that really makes my parents pay attention. "Isn't it supposed to make you not that way?" I say.

"It has the opposite effect on some of us."

"You don't look suicidal," I say. Although when I think about it, there could be thousands of ways to be suicidal.

"Well, don't get too close to me. I could blow at any second." She laughs. There she goes again, taking it so lightly.

But she quickly sobers up. "People think being depressed is just being tired and lazy. It isn't. It's more like being dead when you're still breathing."

I want to hear more, but we've come to the street in front of the school, and I notice the other kids are coming back from the walk. Nina grabs me, and we sneak along behind the trees that line the street until we're at the rear of the gym class.

"I love it when there's a substitute," Nina says.

#

On the way home, Beth is not on the bus. But I don't have to worry too long. She jumps out of the blackberry bushes when I walk by.

"Hey, hey," she says.

"What are you doing?"

"Mom is not ready to meet Dylan, and Dad is definitely not ready. Dylan let me off here and went back to track practice. Isn't that cool? He went way out of his way."

"Cool," I mumble.

We walk in silence for a moment and then I ask, "Do you know what a Renaissance man is?"

"Sure. A Renaissance man is a guy who's good at a lot of different things. Why do you want to know?"

"A girl called me that," I say.

"Hmm," she says. "I wouldn't really think of you as a Renaissance man."

"Well, I guess some people would," I say. And I feel buoyant, even skippy. I take off ahead of her, galloping all the way.

#

Now is not the time to be sneaking out of the house, so I stay in my room and try to keep myself busy. I reach under my bed and pick up the book that is still overdue at the library. I flip through the pages, but my mind is not there.

The good feelings start to go away. And once again, on the inside of my head, something is flexing its muscles. I'm wondering if the rest of my life will always be a fight with myself. Or will The Girl always come and make it all better?

As I think of her, I should be calming down, but my nerves are on fire. All up and down my arms and legs, the synapses spark to life. My brain rolls around like a ball bouncing against my skull. I feel pressure and reach up to touch my head when:

How would you like to have the life of a lifetime, Mr. Renaissance man?

I sit up higher and look around. Another voice I don't know. My tongue suddenly feels thick and tarry. "What?"

Be bold? Be tough? Live the life you should be living?

"I don't know what you mean," I say.

Change it up, then. Make it great. Make them respect you. Before it's too late, Mr. Cammy.

"Who are you?" I cry.

Are you down for a change?

eight

AT dinner, my hands are shaking. Dad notices.

"Something up, bud?"

"Not really," I say. From across the table, Mom smiles nervously at me. "Too much homework maybe." She winks, as if now we're buddies because I told her about my girlfriend.

"I know what that's about," Dad says, laughing. For a moment, he and Mom commiserate about their school days, and Beth sighs big while she stirs her spaghetti with a fork.

"When do I get my phone back?" she asks.

Before the argument gets going, I excuse myself, and I'm back up in my room within minutes. I realize

I'm scared of this new voice. I call him The Other Guy. He has a power that fills all the dark places in my head. The places I usually hide. It's as if there is no hiding from him, and that makes me nervous. I squirm and pace for a few minutes, but my anxiety gets the best of me, and I dive under my blankets. My body is still vibrating when Mom comes up at the usual ten to nine.

"I ended up telling your father about the other morning in the yard," she says as she rests on the side of my bed. "You understand why I had to?"

I shrug. "What did he say?"

"It worries him. He'll probably want to talk to you about it later in private."

Just say your dad should be careful about what he says to you.

"All right," I say instead. Part of me wants to mention the new scary voice to my mom, but I don't trust that she won't go berserk on me. Which is too bad, since sometimes just telling about strange things makes them seem less strange.

"How are you and your girlfriend doing?" she asks.

"Well. You know, okay."

Mom grins and pats my leg through the covers. I can tell she feels good about this. I think now she has a different kind of worry with my girlfriend, but it's one she's been through herself with Dad, and knowing about it must feel comforting to her. She stands up. "I didn't tell your father about the girlfriend part," she says. "Just be careful, okay?"

"I'll try," I say.

When she's gone, the night stretches out long and dense. My thoughts are like a dog without a leash. Dr. Simons once told me the mind is a big house with many corridors and rooms we can explore. But sometimes people get trapped in them, like rats in a maze, and it causes panic. It helps if you have a plan of escape.

The trouble with you is that you're too afraid to speak up. But nothing bad will happen if you do. Try it. You'll see.

I close my eyes tightly, which sometimes makes voices go away. Not tonight.

Seriously. Just show them how tough you really are. Then the tables will turn. They'll be afraid of you.

"Not now," I say. "I want The Girl."

My room is quiet for a moment and then:

Hello, Cam.

I am warmed by her voice, but shiver anyway.

You seem upset.

"I am," I say. "Did you hear what that other guy said?"

Yes. But don't be afraid. We have each other.

I start to relax and feel tingly and begin to understand why Beth is always smiling now that she has a boyfriend.

"You're the only girl who understands me." I flush at how corny I sound.

It's silent again for a while. I think I can actually hear the turning of the earth on its squeaky axis. But it's quiet too long and my gut does a strange flip. "Are you still there?" I try out loud.

Nothing back.

"Please, don't leave," I say more softly.

I do understand you.

I feel a great relief in my lungs. "You're back."

I lie alone, waiting. It is a hopeful feeling I have now. I like having The Girl. The others can go, especially this latest one, but I want her to stay.

I hear a quiet humming in my brain. At first I think it is a crazy buzz, but then I realize it is her. She's humming a lullaby. I think about how she looks, the cut of her hair. I can almost see her fingers clasped around each other. I slowly unwind. Somewhere in the middle of the song, I fall asleep. Having a girlfriend is great.

#

At school, there is a paper heart on my desk, left over from Valentine's Day. I open it and recognize Nina's handwriting, all curlicues and exclamations. "To my partner in crime," it says. I look up and see her teeth on parade.

Mrs. Owens is still sick, but she stands at the front of the class anyway. Her nose is even redder, and now it's peeling. "I think you should practice your reading," she says tiredly. She puts her hands on her desk and slumps into her chair.

Griffin opens his book and stands it on his desk. He hides paper and pen behind it, begins doodling. He starts out with a human head and then adds a cow's hoof sprouting from a lolling tongue. He snorts.

I take my own pen and paper and start to draw. I begin with squares and rectangles, boxy images that don't look right. I cross out the boxes and start drawing more oval shapes. I carefully pen a kind of wave that flows down one side and stops at the bottom of the oval, and then a different one that flows down the other side.

"What is it?" whispers Griffin, who peeks over my shoulder.

I shrug. I am busy creating lips, the top thinner than the bottom.

"Oh, I get it," says Griffin. "It looks like—"

"My girlfriend," I finish for him.

Griffin peeks over at Nina and then back to the drawing.

"Not her," I say. "My girlfriend's hair is short."

"Decent face," Griffin says.

"Thanks," I say.

"Pretty, like Nina," he says. "Same nose and lips."

"But different," I say. I paint in her eyes, big and round and dark. They look up from the page and see only me. I feel a twinge in my heart.

"Nice," says Griffin. But he is not satisfied. "So if she's not Nina, then who is she?"

Mrs. Owens looks up and glares at him, barely shaking her head.

When her eyes close again, I struggle for an answer. But I don't need to because:

I'm just me. People don't always need a name.

"People don't always need a name," I say. Griffin pulls back and eyes me suspiciously. "And she doesn't go to school here," I add.

Mrs. Owens stands up and starts walking slowly around the room. She pauses here and there to look over a student's shoulder. I add to the drawing until she is too close, and then I fold the paper and put it in my backpack. But not before I carefully write "The Girl" in the corner.

\#

On the way home, I fall asleep on the bus, and Roy, the driver, has to shout to wake me up at my stop. I expect to see Beth come out of the blackberries again, but she's not there, and I drag myself all the way up to the house. Not taking meds makes me more tired.

Today was not a bad day except for one thing. I waited and waited to hear more from The Girl, but she's been quiet since class. Now I'm tired and it's not good for me because, as Dr. Simons says, "Do not let yourself get too hungry, angry, lonely, or tired. It only makes things worse."

Mom greets me at the back door, eyes wide, her hands washing in and out of each other. "Where's your sister?" she asks.

"I don't know."

"Wasn't she on the bus?"

"No. I didn't see her."

She grabs me by the shoulders and makes me look at her. "Cameron, do you know something?"

I look into her eyes and see myself reflected back, but all distorted like through a fisheye camera lens. I feel panicky when I can't stop looking at it. "I don't know where she is," I finally say, and manage to break away.

"When I find out where she is . . ." Mom says as I sneak past her and into the house.

I go up to my room and take the drawing out of my

backpack. I lie on my bed against the wall and stare at it. Soon, her lips start to move like a woman's do when she rubs her lipstick around.

Hello, Cam.

"Hey."

I'm glad you told Griffin that I'm your girlfriend. It makes me proud. And you know what makes me prouder? You don't need that medicine. That's what I think is the coolest thing.

I can't help but puff up my chest a little. I reach down and trace my finger around her image. "It's because I'm a Renaissance man."

You sure are. Do you want to do something?

"Okay," I say. "Like what?"

Let's go somewhere where we can be alone.

"We can be alone here." I kiss the tip of my finger and place it on the lips I drew.

You know what I mean, Cam, don't you?

"I get it," I say. "I'm ready." And my body agrees.

I fold the paper even tighter this time and lay it on the floor. I feel buoyant as I slide into the covers. I have a secret that everybody only thinks they know about. And having it makes the world open up a little wider to make room for me.

nine

I AM both happy and scared on the bus the next morning. I'm happy because of my time with The Girl. It looks like she is here to stay. But I'm also scared because The Other Guy is still unfolding and pushing my guts around.

Beth's friends are not on the bus today, so she sits across the aisle, her arms tight against her chest. She stares out the window, but once in a while she glares over at me. She thinks I ratted her out to Mom and that's why she had to endure the humiliation of having Mom come pick her up at the café by the high school where she was sharing an energy drink with Dylan. And then this morning we both had to sit down at the end of the driveway in Mom's car and wait for the bus to come. It looks like Mom is on a divide-and-conquer mission. I worry that Beth might spill the beans about my medicine.

"It's not my fault," I whisper hoarsely.

But Beth only turns her head slowly and frowns at me again.

"I didn't say anything. Honest."

She turns back to the window. Her fingers clench into a fist and then relax.

When I get off the bus, Nina is there, waiting. She takes me by the arm and drags me over by the side of the school. "What's this I hear about a girlfriend?" she asks. Her face is fiery red.

I can only grunt as I fight to get loose from her.

"And another thing. I'm not invisible. I exist. And my name is Nina. You spell it *N-i-n-a*." She pushes me away, but then grabs on to my shirt again and pulls me closer.

"I don't know what . . ."

"And you're welcome for the Valentine card," she adds. "Not that it makes any difference to you." This time she lets me go for good and walks away, smoothing down the sleeves of her shirt. I decide I don't understand any girls except for The Girl.

I start heading for the classroom door, but walk more slowly the closer I get. I feel jumbled and nervous.

I want to crawl inside myself and hide. The weird unfolding in my guts is now tapping on my skull. I look around for a place to hide, but:

She can't talk to you that way.

I freeze in place. "What way?" I ask.

You know. Like she owns you.

"Oh."

Are you in?

I don't know what to say, so I just stand there.

It'll be fun. We'll cause a little trouble.

Confused and scared, I take off running. I head toward the shop class, make a quick sidestep, and disappear behind the building.

Wait up, Mr. Renaissance man.

I speed up. Sometimes I think if I set my mind to it, I can get enough speed to outrun the voices. I hope it works with this one. I don't want him here. Not now.

Pant, pant, pant, big boy. I'm right behind you.

I actually think I can feel The Other Guy nipping sharply at my neck. I try to go even faster. My lungs burn; my heart hammers against my ribs. My legs turn doughy. I race across the football field. Walking students stop and stare at me.

Don't run away. I've got a plan to make you the coolest guy on the planet.

The voice is right at my ear. My legs hurt. I can't catch my breath, think I'll never be able to catch my breath again. I tumble into the woods at the end of the football field and lie gasping in the wet brown needles beneath the evergreens.

#

I feel a huge fullness in my head with every breath. I'm sure I'm going to explode from the inside out. Parts of me will splatter against the tree trunks, and no one will find what's left for days.

"Help!" I call out feebly. "Please help."

I hear a squeaky jog, first at a distance and then getting closer and closer.

I also hear:

Here she comes. Want us to take care of her?

"Go away!" I shout.

I open my eyes and Nina looms over me. "I don't think you really want me to go away, do you?" She too is panting from the run. She bends down and takes my pulse. "What happened to you?" she says.

"Testing," I say breathlessly. "Just testing." The Other Guy seems to have gone.

"Testing what?" She grabs my wrist and pulls me up. Needles cling to my pants.

"How fast I could go," I say. "Could go, could go."

"I think you should test how fast you can stop," Nina says. But she's wary now as she swipes at the needles. From a distance it must look like she's spanking me.

"I can get it," I say. My breathing is still too fast, but it is slowing down. When I'm done cleaning the needles off, we stare at each other.

"So, are you okay?" she asks.

"Maybe."

"Well, are you going back?"

I look toward the school and shake my head. "I don't think so."

"You want to take off, then?"

"Where would we go?"

She points toward town and then uphill and then in another direction. "It's wide open, kid."

I jerk up my backpack so it is steady, and we take off toward town.

We end up at the narrow street that runs beneath the Peter Crawford Bridge. Here the asphalt crumbles, and deep potholes have been bumped out by car tires. The piers of the bridge are mud-caked and shot with graffiti. Nina leads me across the street and down to the water's edge. Big wet rocks are piled up on the shore to keep the river from cannibalizing its own banks. We step up on one and balance ourselves.

The water runs brown and quick. The runoff from Mount Rainier and every other high place is collected in this river and rushes toward the ocean, eighty miles away.

"It smells murky," I say.

"So do you have a girlfriend or not?" she asks.

"Kind of," I say. I've never faced this before, a jealous girl.

"How can you kind of have a girlfriend? That's not possible. You either have one or you don't."

"Then I do."

She is quiet for a moment, then says, "I can't tell you how many times I've felt like jumping off this thing."

"Why would you want to do that?"

She shrugs. "Sometimes I wonder, who do we have to live for? I mean, look at you, Cam. You don't look so hot. And I'm sure I must look like some bad dream. What's the use?"

The important thing is to listen. One can pick up important clues if one opens one's ears. Listening is generally the right thing to do.

"Where have you been?" I ask The Professor.

"I'm right here," says Nina.

`And listen closely.`

I wave The Professor off and Nina notices.

"Are you sure you're okay?" she asks.

"Right now I am."

She sighs and sits on one of the wet rocks. "So you really like her, huh?"

I nod. "Who told?"

"Griffin. He likes to see me suffer."

"She's cool," I say.

"Where does she go?"

"I don't want to talk about it."

"Griffin said she's cute."

"He's never seen her. And the drawing isn't exactly right."

"So there's a chance she could be even cuter?" Her voice is as dark as the mud.

"I said I don't want to talk about it."

"So where is she? Why isn't she here with you?"

"Uh," I murmur. All of a sudden, my footing isn't so sure. "She was busy."

This seems to perk Nina up. "Well, I'm here with you."

I look at her hair. I don't know why I didn't notice it before, but it's not quite dark enough. Her eyes are spaced a little too far apart. Her nose doesn't have the little crook in it I like. Her lips are slightly thicker than I like. And the eyebrows are scary. Then she says something that throws me.

"If you feel like kissing me, don't. I'm not in the mood."

I'm so shocked that I start babbling and can't control it. "Nah-nah-nah-nah-nah," I keep saying.

This amuses her. She laughs so hard, she has to hold on to her stomach. "Nah-nah-nah-nah-nah," she says, mimicking me. "Nah-nah-nah-nah-nah. What a dork."

And deep in my brain, I feel the buildup again, the uncontrollable urge to shout out bad things.

She's mocking you for no reason.

"Stop it," I say.

"Nah-nah-nah-nah-nah." She bends over, as if she'll never be able to stop laughing at me.

But when she finally looks up, maybe Nina sees a change in the tone of my eyes, because she recoils, stumbles back to the rock, and says, "Sorry, I didn't mean to ride you."

I have to steady myself because there is a rush like waves pouring over my brain. As if I'm actually standing on the ocean and one crashes into me and I have nothing to latch on to. I feel dizzy.

"Oh no," I say. I close my eyes tightly and wait for

it to end. When I open them, she is squatting in front of me.

She pulls a handkerchief out of her pocket and dabs it in the standing water between the rocks. She brushes it against my forehead. Then she blows on the spot.

I can feel the water evaporate, and it feels cool and invigorating and temporary, like ice in the desert. But now I'm on edge, waiting for what my brain will do next.

"You should have seen your face go all white," she says. "As if someone plugged a straw into your jugular and sucked all the red out. It was freaky."

"I'm okay now," I lie.

She dabs a little more at my face, and I like how sweet and gentle the motion is.

"Let's go," she says.

"I need to do something," I say. I remember what Dr. Simons once told me. Don't wait too long because then it might be too late. Do something when you're still feeling almost good. I lean down and pick up one of the wet rocks. My eyes burn in the dank underbridge.

Nina takes one look at me holding the big jagged rock and scrambles over the boulders and up to the road.

"No!" I cry, not understanding. But when she's out of sight, I glance down at the rock in my hand and I get it. I was just going to make it splash in the river, but she doesn't trust me. I don't trust me. I drop the rock as if it were a hot coal. Then I walk out from under the bridge.

#

My joints feel rigid and I'm walking like a robot. I've been walking and walking toward Dr. Simons's office. I don't see Nina anywhere.

I guess we showed her.

"I guess," I say.

What are you going to the doc's office for? You know what that means, don't you?

"I just want to find something out, that's all," I say.

Talking gets you nothing. Let's do something unforgettable.

"Like what?"

Pick up a couple of chicks maybe. Something that will make people say, "There goes the coolest guy."

I look up and the clouds look back down at me. They briefly roil into chubby, dark, horrible faces and then quickly disappear into choking swirls of mist. I wouldn't mind being unforgettable, but right now I'd settle for just normal. But how do I do that?

I'm not one to talk, but this trip is definitely forgettable.

Something is breaking down inside my head, and I can almost see my miniature self up there, running around with timbers and a hammer, keeping the walls from caving in. I get one edge secure and hear the crumbling of another. I'm exhausted without even leaving my mind.

I reach the City Circle and put one hand up to defy cars as I walk across the main street and into the park.

"I don't know where I am," I call.

Do it again.

"Do what?"

Pick up a rock. Make them scared. Make them run.

I do not look either way as I cross the street on the other side of the park. An angry driver never quits saluting me with his horn.

Soon he is joined by another, and another. The music of the cars swells up too loud, and I collapse on the street. I wonder if I'll ever have the strength to stand up. Then I am lifted to my feet by a pair of strong hands.

ten

Right from the beginning there is a problem. Dr. Simons's waiting room is packed, and there is no room for Nina to sit down. She stands, with her arms crossed, in the middle of the floor while I try to get in.

"Dr. Simons," I say to the young receptionist behind the desk. "Simons, Simons," I add for good measure.

I think I must be too insistent because her face flames as red as her dress, and I think I've set her on fire.

"Cameron, you don't have an appointment, and he's very, very busy."

"It's incredibly necessary," says Nina.

I glance back at Nina and then bang my head against the counter once, very hard.

The receptionist pushes herself back in her chair, her hand at her throat. "Cameron!"

"Please," I say.

I have to wait until the doctor is done with his current patient and then another fifteen minutes while he does a med check on another. By the time he's done, it's almost lunchtime.

Dr. Simons wears a white lab coat that has three or four writing instruments sticking out of the pocket. "Dr. Simons" is embroidered in blue just below them. He comes out into the waiting room, smiles at a few people still there, pushes back his thinning blond hair, and then blows out a big, tired breath as he takes me by the arm and ushers me to a small room just behind the receptionist.

"What's the problem?" he asks me.

"Have to talk to you."

"It's bad," Nina says from the doorway. "I had to drag him out of the middle of the street."

The doctor glances at her and then scratches his head. "Okay. But I have only a few minutes."

I stand up, and my glare pushes Nina back into the waiting room.

In the doctor's room, I hurry to my favorite gray chair and plop into it. I rest my head against the scratchy fabric.

"Well?" says Dr. Simons.

"I need help."

"Yes?"

"Is it possible to make one voice go away and keep a different one forever?"

One wonders which voices you are talking about.

The doctor has been standing, but now he gently eases himself into his soft black leather chair. "I'm not sure what you're saying," he says.

"I have a girlfriend."

"Okay."

"And I want to keep her. Can you help me?" I bite my tongue so I won't repeat the last sentence. Dr. Simons does not like echolalia.

Although it would not seem erudite to say it, what am I, chopped liver?

"Be quiet," I say.

Dr. Simons raises an eyebrow and then clasps his hands together. "Is that your girlfriend out in the waiting room?"

"No, that's Nina. Just a friend."

"Then who is your girlfriend, Cameron?"

I hesitate to tell him, but he is my therapist. "I don't know her name. And she's out of town. Out of town."

Now the doctor notices the repeat. He scoots his chair over to be closer to me. The squeaky wheels make my head ache. "Can you answer me one question before I help you, Cameron?"

"Okay."

"Have you been taking your Risperdal?"

"Of course," I say, but I can't look the doctor in the face.

"Because it seems like maybe you're not taking them. Your story is not quite right," he goes on. "And look at you. You're wet and dirty, and is it true that the young lady out there had to pick you up off the street?"

I hang my head.

"Cameron?"

"Please don't tell my mom. Please. I don't want to lose my girlfriend."

The doctor puts a soft hand on my shoulder. "Your mother is very devoted to you."

"But she'll make me lose The Girl."

When involved in a discussion such as this, it would be best to include everyone present. Voices are the product of your own thought processes. One could be thinking this through better.

"I see." Dr. Simons heaves a sigh and scoots back over to his desk. His fingers tap the buttons on his phone. "Cameron, you and I go back a long way. I've always tried to do what's best for you. And I'd like to do that now."

I close my eyes tightly and imagine a life without The Girl. "No. Please," I say. But even with my eyes closed, I can hear the doctor's fingers punching the buttons on his phone.

#

I sit in the back examining room that the doctor hardly ever uses. The walls are a bare glaring white. There is a pair of orange plastic chairs facing each other, a small low table between them. I hold a paper cup of water and stare at my reflection in it. Nina came in a half hour before and said goodbye.

Now I hear voices out in the hall, but none I recognize from inside my head. Soon, the doorknob jiggles and my mom comes in. She has that look on her face, the one that tells me I will never stop being the patient in my family.

"Cam," she says. I can hear the tears in her voice, see the red in her eyeballs.

Behind her, Dad looms in the doorway. The top of his head barely fits through. He has his work clothes on. On his shoulder, a dark stain from the machine at the mill looks like the map of Texas. "What's up, son?" he says. "Too much homework?"

But I can't answer him. Mom has mashed my face into her chest. I can barely breathe. I finally have to push her away. She takes my chin in her hands and studies me.

"I knew it," she says. "Didn't I ask you about the meds?"

Shut up.

Dr. Simons comes through the door. "Ah, I see we're all here," he says. "It seems we have a little problem."

"Not one that can't be fixed," says my dad. He walks over to me but doesn't stop. He ends up doing a circle and standing a few feet away.

"I don't understand it," Mom says. "Things were going so well and now this." She shakes me a little. "Weren't things going well?"

You touch me one more time . . .

I don't want to answer. I don't want to tell her that her mouth is making big ballooning motions as she talks.

"He's fourteen," says Dad. "Fourteen-year-olds like to do things like this."

"We could speculate until the sun goes down," says Dr. Simons, "but that doesn't change the fact that this young man is in trouble." He turns toward me. "Are you hallucinating, Cameron?"

"No."

"Are you sure?"

"Yes. I don't see anything weird."

"But what about the voices? You've had trouble with voices before."

My dad turns away. He doesn't like to hear this kind of talk. I've seen it make his gut contract and force him to reach in his pocket for the cigarettes he quit smoking five years ago. He stares out at the parking lot.

"No voices," I repeat.

"The Girl?" says Dr. Simons.

"Who's that?" my mom asks. Then she shakes me again. "Who's The Girl?"

You don't have to take this, you know.

"I told you already," I say.

"Apparently he has a girlfriend," Dr. Simons says. He waits until he has Mom's attention, then does a little head shake and a frown.

But I see it. "She *is* my girlfriend," I insist.

"Of course she is, sweetheart," says Mom.

Of course she is, sweetheart.

I smirk, even though it is The Other Guy. Maybe he's not so bad.

"Well, girlfriend or not, we still have a problem," Dr. Simons says. "It looks like Cameron is in quite a bit of distress. My suggestion is we give him a shot today and find him a bed at Saint John's so he can sleep it off."

"I don't want a shot," I cry.

A shot will clear up the confusion.

"And end up killing you," I say.

My.

"So, yes, in answer to your previous question, you are chopped liver," I say.

This seems to scare my dad. "You have to have a shot right now," he says.

And that is what happens. Dr. Simons leaves, and pretty soon the nurse comes in carrying a tray with a hypodermic needle resting on it. She has me roll up my sleeve, dabs my skin with alcohol, and then pierces it with the needle.

Cam, what are you going to do about this?

I watch the serum go into my arm, thinking this is what they do when they execute someone. I wince, but it isn't from the pain. I can hear The Girl pleading.

What's going on, Cam? It hurts.

"You're killing her," I cry to the nurse.

Don't let them do this, Cam. Please.

"Hold on, young man," the nurse says.

Please, Cam. I don't want to die. I love you.

I stand up, trying to pull away while The Girl's voice sounds like it's drifting into nothingness, but the nurse is already finished. She rubs at the spot again and then takes away her tray. I suddenly feel so flushed that I have to sit down. My head swarms with smoky clouds. I imagine special forces with machine guns, seeking out all the unwelcome guests in my head and killing them.

"That'll hold him," the nurse says at the door.

"I want to go home," I say.

#

But I don't get to go there yet.

I mostly sleep. The shot has gone straight to my brain and cut off everything. I can't feel sad or happy or mad or enlightened. Only tired. I wake up every couple of hours and try to make sense of the hospital room. But it is dark even though it is still day, and my eyes close to keep my wobbly head from falling over. I hear other voices in the room, the chiming of bells.

I don't dream. I don't dance through the halls with The Girl. I don't sneak out of the house and find my own place. There is no one with me.

When I wake up for good the next morning, I'm exhausted from all the sleep. At first I can't feel the ends of my arms. My hands seem to be floating above the blankets.

A nurse pads in on her velvety white shoes. She has copper hair, and a stethoscope has created a faint black ring around her neck. She pumps up my arm and then listens to the beating of my heart. I imagine she can tell that it's broken.

"Are you there?" I croak out words, but my throat is too relaxed from not talking, and I end up coughing.

"I'm here." The nurse waits for more with the stethoscope dangling.

But she's not the one I want to hear from. "I'm hungry," I finally say.

"He speaks," the nurse says. Then she digs into her pocket and pulls out a saltine cracker. "Here."

I grab it and spend a few seconds trying to tear apart the cellophane before I bite into the cracker. My mouth is immediately flooded with salt and I moan.

"I'll get you a menu," she says, and is gone as silently as she showed up.

#

At home, there is a knock on my bedroom door. "Cam? It's Mom." She's been in and out since I got back.

She opens the door and enters with a tray. Something steams from a bowl in the center of it. She sets it down on the table to let it cool.

"Now I want you to tell me the truth," she says. "How long did you stop taking your medicine for?"

I shake my head.

"You don't want to talk?"

I shake it again.

Mom sighs and her shoulders sag. "I wish there was a way to get through to you." She reaches out and pats my covers. "Cam, I know you've lived with it and so you understand, but I just want to tell you again."

Everything she says makes my head hurt.

"This is very, very serious. You have an illness that you can't play around with. You have to treat it with respect. You respect it and it respects you. I know it scares you when it gets out of hand; you've told me that before. If you don't want to be afraid, there is one way that you can make the fear go away. And that's by taking your medicine the way you're supposed to. This is what happens if you don't take it. Do you understand that? Of course you do."

I find my voice among the pile of debris in my mouth. "It's you who doesn't understand," I say.

"What do you mean?"

"It's not worth it to tell you. You just don't get it."

"Try me," she says.

I actually consider telling her everything, to start over fresh, but the look on her face tells me she can't take it.

"Please?" she says.

I turn from her. "Just go away," I say.

eleven

No school for me yet and it's like being grounded.
I'm propped up on the couch with a blanket over me.
The TV is on a twenty-four-hour news station. I've
heard the same news about the Middle East for the past
two hours. I reach for the remote, but it's as if my mom
has new ears. She pops into the family room. "Is there
something you need, sweetie?"

"No."

"Anything I can bring you?"

My own life, I think, but I don't say it.

"You'll let me know?" She nods. She's really trying,
I know, but she is more than annoying.

"Leave," I say.

She actually smiles. "You know how I can tell when you're getting better? When you start acting like a teenager."

I ignore her.

"Okay," she whispers.

There is nothing to my life now. I rub at the spot where the nurse took away everything. Before that, even though I had the voices, I was at least feeling something. Now I can't feel anything. I try to force myself to laugh, but can't. To cry, but can't. I pinch the skin on the top of one hand, but don't care.

By the afternoon, I dress myself and walk aimlessly around the house. In every room I end up in, there is my mother pretending to clean. I imagine her as a hallucination, but it doesn't work. I chew on the inside of my cheek until I can taste blood. I notice that Mom smiles more now, seems happier. She is cleaning in a way I've never seen her do before. She even polishes the same table twice and then a third time. When she's through, she stands and looks at me, a drop of sweat trickling down her face.

"Just like the old days," she says. "Remember before you went to school you used to follow me around the house?"

"No," I say, although I do.

"You used to carry the spray bottle for me. You

were my little helper. Then we'd sit down and watch *As the World Turns* together. You could tell me everything that was going on with all the characters."

"I don't remember," I lie. But I close my eyes and picture it. There is a TV tray in front of me, and every time I lean down to take a spoonful of soup, I jiggle the tray and it spills. Mom sits next to me with a roll of paper towels and reaches over every time, her eyes glued to the TV, and wipes up the spill.

I open my eyes again and Mom is staring. Her eyes glimmer with tears. "I wish I could help you," she says.

"Then stay out of my business," I grumble.

I can see this shocks her. I've closed the communication window that she has spent the day trying to open. Slammed it on her hand. "What have I done?" she asks.

"You killed my girlfriend," I say.

"Oh, Cameron—"

"Don't 'Oh, Cameron' me," I shout. "I had her and now she's gone. And you're the one who took her away."

Her mouth hangs open as she struggles to say something. "Cameron, this girl isn't real. Am I wrong about that? If I am, I would dearly love to meet her."

"She doesn't want to meet you," I say. "She doesn't even like you."

"How can she make a judgment about me if we've never met?"

"Because I told her," I blurt out. "I told her how mean and uncaring you are."

Now Mom's face crumbles, and she fights to keep from falling apart. The tears ease their way down her cheeks. I watch one as it rolls along, like a raindrop on a window glass. I'm intrigued and step in closer to watch it.

"Why do you have to be this way?" Mom asks. "Why do you have to make me cry?"

I hear a crashing in my head, as if all my caged emotions are bumping off each other at once. Mad crashes into happy, and sad bounces off of guilty until they all lie in a big smoky heap in my mind.

"I haven't done anything wrong," she wails, but I'm busy trying to snatch each of those words out of the air and throw them back at her. I manage to snag *done* and *wrong*, but the rest of them float up to the ceiling and out of my grasp.

#

I mourn in my bed as warm air blows gently from the vent. I reach under my pillow and pull up the doodles I did of The Girl. I touch them with my finger but don't feel anything back. I got mad at my mom, so at least I have one feeling, but I want something different.

Love maybe? Why can't I have that? Isn't it normal for someone my age? I just know it's the meds that keep me from love.

There are layers in my head, and I can almost see them, like levels of sedimentary rock exposed on a cliff. Layers of fear and pain and Mom and Dad and Beth and The Professor and The Girl and a sinister layer right beneath her: The Other Guy. He seems way down in a place I've never gotten to. I liked how he talked to my mom, but I'm afraid I haven't heard all of him yet, and that makes me feel shaky. Thinking of these things, I can't sleep and roll around like a ball in the bed of a rambling pickup truck.

The heat whispers on and off all through the night. I start to worry, which is a good sign. I need to figure out a way to get my girlfriend back. Finally, at three in the morning, darkness covers my brain and lets me be for a few hours.

twelve

My mom makes me eat oatmeal the next morning. "It'll stick to your ribs," she says. I eat it slowly, but leave a tiny mound like a molehill in the middle of the bowl.

"Am I going to school today?" I ask. I think about what I must face when I get there. Everyone knows now. News like mine travels fast.

"That depends on how you feel," she says.

I must choose between another day with my mom or facing the music at school.

"I don't know," I say.

She walks over and puts an arm around my shoulder. I can smell soap. "You don't have to go," she says.

"I'll go," I quickly say.

"But the bus has already come," she says.

"You can take me." And before she can say anything, I've bounded back up the stairs to my room.

\#

Mom goes to the school office with me. We wait a few minutes for Mr. Rudy, the vice principal, who comes bustling in. He has buttoned his blazer wrong, and it hangs, bunched and lopsided, off his belly. Coffee has spilled on his white shirt, and I count four oblong brown droplets.

"Always a pleasure," Mr. Rudy says.

I wonder briefly what could be the difference between Mr. Rudy's voice and the ones I hear in my head. He would fit in easily as a character in *Alice in Wonderland*.

We squeeze into Mr. Rudy's office and sit opposite his desk. From the corner of my eye, I can see what's going on in the rest of the offices.

"First of all," Mom says, "I need to inform you that Cameron has had another episode, and that's why he hasn't been at school. I called Mrs. Johnson earlier . . ."

"Yes, yes," says Mr. Rudy. "I received that message." He turns to me and speaks over the top of his steepled fingers. "I'm sorry to hear about your problem," he says.

I shrug but stay quiet.

Mom sends her eyes to the ceiling. "You'll have to forgive him," she says. Then she raises one eyebrow.

"Quit that," I say.

But Mom misinterprets. "See what I mean?" she says in a whisper.

Mr. Rudy nods. "But before we continue, I do have a question." This time he turns his whole body toward me and rests an elbow on the desk. "Do you happen to know where Nina Savage is?"

"Oh, Lord," Mom says.

But Mr. Rudy puts a hand up to stop her. "Cameron?"

"She's not in class?" I say.

"No. And she hasn't been during the week you've been out. I was hoping you could shed some light on this mystery."

"Maybe she's home."

"No one answers the phone or the door at her residence."

"Maybe they decided to go on vacation."

"It's just that she was last seen with you," says Mr. Rudy.

"Oh no," says my mom, throwing herself back in her chair. "Cameron, if you know anything at all about this girl, you'd better start talking."

"I don't," I say. But I wonder.

Later, Mrs. Johnson escorts me to class. Mrs. Owens seems glad to see me, and Griffin is full of questions. As I sit down, I see that Nina's chair is vacant.

"Went loony, huh?" whispers Griffin. "Wish I would someday. They say it's cheaper than drugs. Is it cool, Cam? I mean, when you go off the deep end?"

I just stare at him until he turns away. But he'll bug me again soon, and I feel a burning frustration grow in my stomach. I throw up my hand and get up before Mrs. Owens calls on me. "I have to go to the bathroom," I say, and I leave the room before she can grant me permission.

I veer away from the boys' and head down the hall. I feel a fierce determination. Nothing can get in my way. I think I see Mrs. Johnson standing in the hall, but I don't stop to confirm it. Instead, I power through the front door and out into the parking lot.

A few cars are parked there, but no one is around. I hurry across the lot and run to the other side of the street when I see a car coming. I figure out what I will say if someone tries to stop me from going farther.

Just try to stop me, I think. But no one does, and I move on to the little red house not far from the market.

I stand in front of it for a moment. I hear nothing and see only a black and white cat sitting, tail curled, on the front steps. I walk up the driveway and stand under the rotting carport. It smells wet and musty. I knock on the side door and wait. I knock again. "Nina?" I try the door, and the knob twists coolly in my fingers.

Well, well. Aren't we the little juvenile delinquent.

The voice throws me back. I stumble and struggle to stay upright. "Please," I whisper. The rule is that I don't hear voices so soon after a shot. But this guy isn't following the rules. Something must be wrong.

Breaking and entering. I like this.

"Stop it," I say, and gently push the door open.

The laundry room smells strongly of neglected cat, and it takes a moment for me to get used to it. I push myself against the door and close it. The chipped linoleum beneath my feet gives as I walk across it and into the tiny kitchen.

Old dishes wait to be done up in the sink. Plastic wrappers and an old greasy pizza box litter the counter. I smell something else in the air that reminds me of a few days in the hospital. Something that just plays with my senses, inviting me to explore further, to peek around the next corner.

To the side of the refrigerator, the room opens into a short hallway. I stand for a few seconds and scratch at my cheek. One foot gets courageous, but the other wants to grow roots.

"Nina?" I say.

The other foot finally loosens and I move into the hall. A few feet away a door stands open. A circle of watery light shines off a window. Below it, I see Nina in a T-shirt and boxers, her body spread out awkwardly on a bed. She is as still as a corpse. My breathing halts.

"Nina?"

I step into the doorway. "Oh God," I say right before Nina bolts off the bed as if she's just been stung. She tries to pull the blanket around her, but it won't move.

"Get out!" she screams. "Get out!"

Her words are like gale-force winds and push me away from the door. I stumble against the jamb, right myself, and hurry back to the kitchen. I lean against the sink, breathing hard.

She's not shouting now, and I wait for some other noise. Pretty soon, she comes out.

"What are you doing here, you pervert!" she says.

I flee out the back. I'm already on the street before she can swing open the front door.

"Wait! Cameron! Wait!"

I stop and turn toward her. But as I do:

Be a man, Cammy. She'll only try to get in your head.

Now I fear what I might do. "I don't want to hurt you," I say, and as she steps down to the grass, I add, "Stop right there. Or . . ."

"What's wrong?" she asks.

"The rules have changed," I say.

Nina cocks her head. "How?"

"Don't ask me how, but he's back. The guy from under the bridge."

Nina nods. I search for some bigger reaction on her face but don't find it. "He went away and now he's back?"

I check for The Other Guy, but my head is quiet. "They shot me up," I say. "They took it all away."

She puts her hands on her hips. "Life sucks."

#

"I'm sorry about sneaking in on you," I say. "And about, you know, kind of threatening you just now."

She stretches her back. "I wasn't scared, Cam. Just surprised. I trust you."

"You do?" I feel a nub of heat start up in my gut, and it turns into a blaze. "It's all good," I say.

"That's what I like to hear," she says.

But it's something else that has me excited. If The

Other Guy has shown up, what's to keep The Girl from being here also? "Hey," I say. "Hey."

"Hey back," Nina says. She tries to take my hand, but I'm moving around too much.

I walk farther out in the street, trying to concentrate.

"Cam?"

I'm turning in a circle. Whose voice was that?

I feel Nina come up behind me. Her touch gives me goose bumps. I turn around and grab her arms. "You're the best," I say, and feel the good words course through my body.

"Let's go inside," she says. She snags my hand and tries to pull me.

But I take my hand back. "They're going to come looking for me," I say. And I take off running down the street.

thirteen

BACK at school, I'm relieved that Mrs. Owens has not called anybody about my absence.

"I really had to go," I insist, and she reluctantly accepts my excuse.

"You know you have a doctor's appointment this afternoon," she says as she unlocks a cabinet beneath the work counter on the side of the classroom. She peeks in and pulls out a paper cutter. "Your mother will be here to pick you up at two o'clock." I must look worried, because Mrs. Owens touches my arm gently. "It's okay, Cameron," she says. "You'll feel so much better afterward."

I see right then that even the good people don't really understand. But I still try to convince them anyway.

"I wish I didn't need a crutch, Mrs. Owens," I say.

"And I'm sure that's what everyone wants for you too." She raises the curved sharp handle of the cutter and places ten sheets of colored paper beneath it. I have an image of a guillotine and shudder as she brings the blade down, severing all the sheets cleanly.

"Are you happy?" I ask.

"Me? Yes, of course." But I don't believe her. I see her eyes dart away too quickly. She hurriedly places more paper beneath the blade and grabs the handle.

"You don't look happy," I say.

"Looks can be deceiving," she says, and brings the blade down in a hard swift movement that makes me jump again even though I knew it was coming. It loosens something up in my brain.

Nobody gets you.

"I know," I say out loud.

Mrs. Owens pauses with the blade in her grasp, and I have to think quickly.

"Can I go to the library?" I say.

#

Mom pulls up into the lot at precisely two o'clock. Not 1:59 or 2:01. She doesn't see me until I'm right next to the window.

"You shouldn't scare people like that," she says as I slide in and she puts the car in gear.

"People shouldn't be scared," I say. Already my shoe is tapping out the anxiety I feel whenever I go to see Dr. Simons.

Something starts curving up inside me like the blade on Mrs. Owens's machine. It beckons me with its threatening shine. I glance secretly at my mother. Her hands are solid on the wheel, her eyes unwavering on the road. Little does she know that one of the voices has come back so soon. And if one of them has come back, that means . . .

"I don't want to do this," I suddenly say.

"Cameron . . ."

"I'm fine," I nearly shout out. "I don't need it."

"You do need it," she says back. "You can't be trusted to take the pills."

I wait through two red lights before I say, "But what if I don't need the pills? What if this is just my normal way of being?"

"Cam, it can't be normal to hear and see the things you hear and see." Her voice is more modulated again, like something coming out of a hospital intercom.

"Maybe not for you," I say. "Maybe not for Dad and Beth. But for me, maybe it's a different kind of normal."

I spy on her again and see that she is struggling.

"Nobody knows for sure," I continue. "Even Dr. Simons says nobody really knows what normal is."

"Cam!" she says sharply. "I don't want to talk about this. We're going to Dr. Simons's office, and you're going to get a shot. That's all there is to it."

I lean back against the seat and fold my arms. "We'll just see about that," I say.

#

At 2:35 we are in Dr. Simons's office. We haven't exchanged words since the fight in the car. I am sitting in the big leather chair, and I swing it back and forth while we wait. My mom holds her paperback in front of her.

Soon, Dr. Simons walks in. Pens are perched behind each of his ears, and he carries one in his hand. "Hello," he says cheerfully.

"Hello, Doctor," says my mom. She puts down the book and smiles.

"Well now," Dr. Simons says when he sees I'm in his chair.

"Let the doctor sit," says my mom.

But I stay put and the doctor says, "It's okay. Really." He takes a wheeled chair nearby and rolls over to me. "Well now, how are we doing?"

"Not good," I say.

"Better," Mom says.

Dr. Simons looks from me to her and then back again.

"He's not all manicky," my mom says.

"Is that true?" asks the doctor.

"Do we know what normal is?" I ask.

Dr. Simons scratches his chin. "Well, we know what normal isn't, if that helps."

"You see?" my mom chirps.

I get up from the chair and start pacing the room. Dr. Simons follows me with his eyes. He is used to this, used to figuring out what is going on with his patients simply by observation. I stop at his fish tank and tap a couple of gourami away from the glass.

"He doesn't want to take his shot today," says my mom. "We've had a few words about it."

"Hmm-hmm," murmurs Dr. Simons. "How are the voices, Cameron?"

"You lied," I spit out. "You told me once that nobody really knows what normal is."

"They don't," the doctor agrees. "Normal is different for different people."

"See?" I say back to my mother.

"He's been like that since I picked him up," she says. "Like a smart aleck."

"Frankly, that seems normal to me," says the doctor. "He is, after all, fourteen."

"See?" I say again.

"He's driving me absolutely crazy," my mom says.

"It's hard," the doctor agrees.

While Mom is busy trying not to cry, I try desperately to get the doctor's attention. When I do, I whisper, "Please don't make me take another shot. Please. I don't need it. I don't have any more voices. Please."

My mom suddenly jerks her hands from her face. "Cameron, I am your mother, and I make the decisions about what's good for you. And I think getting a shot is what's best for you. Therefore, you will be getting a shot today. When you reach the age of eighteen, then *you* can decide."

She finally says the thing I've been waiting for her to say. Now I can tell them what Nina helped me learn in the library. "Not exactly," I say.

"What do you mean, not exactly?" she asks.

"In the state of Washington, the age of consent for mental stuff is thirteen."

I look quickly at Dr. Simons and then back over to my mom.

"What are you talking about?" she says. "That's preposterous. A thirteen-year-old can't consent to this."

"Oh yes, he can," I say.

My mom rolls her eyes and says, "Dr. Simons, will you please set him straight?"

"Actually, he's right."

"But kids Cameron's age can't make that important a decision. They're not mature enough."

"In some ways, I agree with you. For example, if they are at risk of doing harm to themselves or others. But otherwise they can."

"But he lives under our roof," my mom complains. "He lives by our rules."

"I understand that," the doctor says. "And that's a different issue." He starts rubbing his fingers rapidly. "All I'm saying is that if you were in a court of law, the law would say Cameron can make up his own mind."

"But look at his mind—" Mom starts to say, but realizes it's mean and clamps her mouth shut.

"I am perfectly okay," I say. "Really, I am. Whatever it was that caused that thing to happen is all gone now."

"Cameron," says Dr. Simons. "We really need to talk about this. You are aware that you have been a sick young man, and this disease is not likely to remit so quickly."

"Yes."

"And we talked before about how this could get out of hand for you again and how the best thing for you may be to have a consistent medication regimen to keep it under control."

I nod. "The earlier you catch it, the less severe the symptoms are."

"Well, I might as well not be here," my mom says, getting up from her chair. She heads for the door, already pulling the cell phone out of her pants and pushing buttons.

When she is gone, Dr. Simons faces me. "This is very serious business you're involved in here, Cameron. Very serious."

"I know," I say. "But I don't want any more shots. They make me feel like I'm not a real person. I don't want to feel weird anymore."

Dr. Simons smiles and scratches above his ear. "I understand what you're saying. But you know who your mother is talking to out there? Your father. I predict he will come home from work early today to have a conversation with you about this. He will try to talk you out of your decision."

"Is it really true, Doctor, what I said? That I can make up my own mind?"

"Yes, it is ultimately true, Cameron. But with it comes a great responsibility. The state is asking you to take the best care of yourself that you possibly can. Do you feel up to doing that?"

I nod again. "And then some."

"Here's what I'd like to do. I'd like to keep prescribing you the medication. You seem reasonably good right now, so I won't insist that you have an injection.

But I want you to continue to take the pills. Will you do that for me, Cameron?"

I bring my fingers up to my chin.

Sometimes adults are almost too easy.

"It will show you're willing to take the responsibility necessary to keep this thing under control," the doctor says. "And it will help calm down your parents."

"Sure I will," I say, hoping my face is as straight as it can be. I stand up to shake the doctor's hand. When I leave, I can almost feel the clouds leaving my head. And now, I'm floating on them.

fourteen

ALL the way home, Mom cannot stop talking about how if my dad hadn't been training a new guy, he would have come home early and set my thinking straight. She says she is going to ask around and see if she can find a different therapist for me, one who appreciates the needs of the parents as well. All the while, I look out the window and think the day is sunnier than normal.

Dr. Simons is right about the pills, though. When we get home and I stand on my side of the car and uncap the little amber bottle, shake one out in my hand, and then throw it to the back of my throat, it does seem to soothe Mom.

"Do you want me to keep track of those for you?" she asks, holding out her hand.

"No," I say. "The doctor says I need to do it myself."

Her eyes narrow, and I can see her chewing on the inside of her cheek, but she goes in the house without saying another word, and that in itself spells victory as I spit the pill onto the driveway and grind it with my shoe.

I take off toward the barn. As I climb, I think winning the battle with my mom has made me more philosophical. Maybe each of us can live only inside our heads, and that's the reason we can't always get along because our world looks different from the world of the guy next to us. And maybe it's a waste of time to try to explain our world to the next person because he'll just never really get it.

"Live a day inside my brain," I say out loud.

I am tramping through my brain and the high weeds so much that I lose track of time, and that is why my dad surprises me when he comes sneaking up on me.

"What do we have here?" he asks. He still wears his blue baseball cap and his dirty work jeans. Dust has collected on the oily surface of his steel-toed boots.

"Hanging," I say.

"Looks to me like you might be talking to some-body who's not there," Dad says, his eyebrows lifting.

"I know Mom's mad at me," I say, getting the jump on him.

"Yeah, she gave me an earful. Is it true what she says? Have you gone and decided to stop with the meds?"

"No," I say.

"I can barely see you, Cam. Come on out of there." He steps back as I wade through the grass. Then he whistles when he sees my clothes are soaked.

"I'm just—"

"Do you even care if you catch pneumonia?"

Him too?

"Dad."

"Cam?"

"I do care and I don't," I say.

Dad looks like I stepped on his last nerve. "You want my opinion? Never mind, you're going to get it anyway. My opinion is that you don't mess with your head. If it's soft, you wear a helmet. It's the most pre-cious thing you've got. You take chances with it and come up wrong, it's a permanent loss. You can't go around as if nothing matters. That's what I think." He twists on his heel and takes off. Right before he turns at the barn, he stops and waves me over. "She's a mess, Cameron. I want you to go apologize to her."

"I'm coming," I say.

I always feel small next to my dad, but most times it doesn't matter. Now it does. I feel his big, looming presence as we stop under the apple tree. Dad looks up into the branches. "I want you to promise me one thing, Cam," he says. "I want you to promise me you won't let it get all out of control."

"I promise," I quickly say.

"No. I mean, really promise, not just say something to get me off your back. The last thing I want is your mother to get hurt."

"Yes," I say vigorously. "I promise."

My dad looks like he's about to go, but he changes his mind. "Do you think it's possible you could be over all this soon?" he asks.

"I want it to be over, Dad."

Dad looks to the distant field past the barn. "I don't understand it, that's all," he says. "I mean, we're good people. We try to do the right thing. That's true, isn't it? I mean, you haven't been doing things in secret like killing animals and skinning them out behind the barn, have you?"

"No, Dad."

"You're not doing drugs, are you?"

Might be.

"Dad."

"I didn't think so." He shakes his head. "I wish they could find the answer to this thing."

"I promise," I say again.

He looks at me with one eyebrow raised. "Maybe the next time I go to the gym you could tag along with me."

"I could try," I say.

Now Dad smiles and reaches out, rubbing the top of my head. "Get down there and apologize," he says.

"Okay," I say.

On my way to the house, I hear:

One shouldn't be so certain about a voice one doesn't really know.

"What do you mean by that?"

I mean, a path that seems clear can very soon become tangled.

"I'm getting kind of tired of you," I say.

#

At school, Nina and I reach the lunch table just ahead of Griffin. He tries to sit next to us, but I block him. "Nina wants to talk to just me," I say.

Nina nods and Griffin sits at the next table facing us. He wears a big frown and I feel guilty.

But Nina and I had that moment at her house, and today I want only her. "I'm glad you're back," I say to her. She looks different, brighter and happier somehow.

"Me too," she says. She cocks her head to one side. "You don't look like a guy who had a shot yesterday."

"I'm not," I say happily.

She nods her approval. "Good one, my man. You're actually growing a pair."

I bite into a pig in a blanket and then tell her how I talked Dr. Simons into doing what I wanted.

"You're getting brave," she says. "Forget about a pair; I think you grew three of them."

A piece of bread bounces off my head, and I look over to see Griffin grinning.

"Please, Griff," Nina says without turning.

"Maybe it's a good thing for us," I say. "It's our bodies. It's our brains. Shouldn't we be able to do what we want with them? Even my dad says we have to do what's best for our heads."

A smile breaks on her face. "You know, you and I make a pretty good team."

"A pretty good team," I say.

fifteen

THE next day at school, Nina and I sneak down the hall toward the central office. Here, as always, the regular students are making their way to their next classes. We pause at the corner and watch them.

"They don't look too different from the kids in our class," Nina says.

Although today I'm not afraid of them, I do feel for the first time a kind of envy. Maybe, I think, maybe someday I can walk among them.

"At my last school, I was in the regular classes," Nina says.

"How was it?"

"Better than anything," she says. "I mean, the kids

are still the same jerks, but for me it was nice just knowing I was one of them."

"So how come you're not still one of them?" I ask.

She turns and starts walking back to our class. "You already know the answer to that."

At lunch, Nina and I quickly eat and then go outside. The air is cool and humid, but it hasn't rained for hours. Groups of students walk around the parking lot; some stand in small knots, talking. Here and there, a single student sits on the steps, reading. It is not common for kids in my class to join in, but I feel different now.

"You want to?" I say. And it's as if she knows what I'm saying.

So we start walking around the lot. When we finish one lap, we end up near our classroom.

"You want to do another?" Nina asks me.

"Nah."

"You want to go out to the track?"

I look out past the wood shop. "Okay."

We walk slowly, and when we've gone behind the shop, Nina slips her arm into mine. I look down on it but don't say anything. We reach the rubberized track. It feels cushiony below my shoes.

"Can I ask you something?" Nina asks. "Have you heard from that girl lately?"

"No," I say.

Her body relaxes next to mine. She hooks her arm in closer.

"She doesn't talk all the time?"

"Not really."

"That might not be a bad thing," she says. "But sometimes I wish I had someone to talk to. I know I can talk to you, but I mean, all the time. Even when I'm at home."

I think about The Girl and try to remember the last time we talked. I can't. The only one I've heard from lately is The Other Guy. Even though I'm with Nina, I now feel lonely. Why can't the good times last longer?

"But I really like the times we talk to each other," Nina continues. "It's just good to have a best friend. Funny that it turns out to be a boy. I have a problem making friends with girls. Do you have a problem making friends with boys?"

"Except for Griffin, I don't make friends with anybody very well."

"Do you think . . ." Nina starts to say, then clears her throat and continues. "Do you think we could maybe go out sometime?"

I stop. "What do you mean?"

"Come on, Cam. Don't make me ask twice. Just answer the question."

"Well." I've never been faced with this question before and it tugs. "You know. I already have a girlfriend."

Nina pulls on me and we start walking again. "Cameron, don't take this wrong, but because we're such good friends, I can say this. You and I both know she's not real."

I walk on, dejected. Something about what Nina says seems like treason. "Your reality is not my reality," I say.

"I'm sorry. I didn't mean anything by it." She jerks on my arm a little to try to get me to laugh, but I walk stiffly around the track until the buzzer sounds for the end of the lunch hour.

As we walk toward the back door, two of the regular girls spy us, arm in arm. "Hey, look at the love nuts," one of them says.

#

The rest of the afternoon, I sit in class, trying to make my head stay clear. I have important questions to ask The Girl, such as what is Nina doing asking me out; why does she want to walk around as if she's my girlfriend; and why is it that kids need to say things like those girls said to Nina and me.

Nina turns and raises her eyebrows. Now I think her eyebrows are very pretty. She quickly scribbles something down and passes it to me.

Forget what those stupid pigs said, it says.

I write back, *Okay.*

Griffin is missing when Mrs. Owens comes into class. She glances at me and I feel the heat.

"I think we need to have a little talk," she says to the whole class. When everyone is settled, she leans against the side of her desk. "I know it's hard for everyone to know that you are members of this class. I told you that on the first day. I hear what other students say, and I think I know how it feels on the inside when you hear it. But please, don't allow that to make wrong decisions for you. Please. Those of you who take medications take them for a reason. They keep you as healthy as possible. If you decide that medications are not for you, that may not be what's best. I've called Griffin's parents, and they will be taking him home. He needs a rest."

We nod our heads as a unit. We've been through this before. At least once a month, one of us is sacrificed to the gods of reason.

"Is it safe?" asks the little rabbit girl in the back of the class. She barely rises above the top of her desk and wrinkles her nose like a bunny.

"Of course it's safe, Amy," says Mrs. Owens. "There's nothing wrong."

"It seems like there's something wrong," Amy answers back.

"Griffin's freaking," Nina says.

"Now, Nina," says Mrs. Owens. "Let's try to use correct language, shall we?"

"*Freaking* is part of the language," Nina says.

Mrs. Owens lets out a big, long breath and crosses her arms. "I think you know what I mean, Nina."

They go on for a minute, but I try to block them out. I don't like banter. It makes claws in my brain that scrape against my skull. Their voices start out strong but now are like ants' voices. One ant arguing with another. I can't take it anymore. I track the words as they rise out of my stomach like a hot geyser and then spew forth.

"He's just trying to be who he really is!" I shout. "That's all!"

The whole class quiets down. Mrs. Owens's face drains of color. Nina turns in her seat and wrinkles hers. The little rabbit girl cowers under her desk.

"Cameron?" Mrs. Owens tries cautiously.

"That's all," I say, more quietly.

#

If you are a danger to yourself or others, then it is not a good idea to take your life into your own hands.

I have read in the library about what he is saying, but I prefer to ignore The Professor's advice. I am different from Griffin. I can handle this taking my life into my own hands. I am excited. Two voices back and one to go. And she is the one I can't wait to hear from again.

But this time it has to be different. This time I have to be careful and smart. If I am, then I can have a girlfriend who loves only me. I can stop taking my meds. I can act like the kids in the regular classes. Other kids will respect me. And I can kiss all this craziness goodbye.

A spark has ignited in me that will never be put out. I can make up my own mind.

sixteen

WHEN I wake up, I feel like I'm in a straitjacket. The covers are wound around me, and my chin is practically touching one knee. I'm a giant version of what grows inside an egg. I suck in a deep breath and then another before I unravel and stand on my bedroom floor.

I wander out in the hall and pause at the top of the stairs. When I look down, they seem to get smaller and smaller and never end. It's scary and I hoof it to the bathroom.

I stand in front of the mirror and study myself under the low, buzzing fluorescent light. It makes my skin look pale and sickly. The whites of my eyes are clotted here and there with tiny yellow yolks.

My life is in my own hands now. Every move I make, it seems like I have to really think it through. When I stand in front of the toilet with the Risperdal in my hand, do I flush it down, or do I pop it in my mouth? I wasn't expecting this dilemma. Isn't freedom supposed to feel free? Just before the water goes swishing away, I drop the pill in.

I hear the phone ring downstairs, and in a moment Mom calls up to me. "Cam! It's that girl!"

I hold my breath as a wave of pleasure washes over me. That girl? I forget my fears for a moment, break out of the bathroom, and drum down the stairs in my boxers. Mom holds the phone out, a frown hanging on her lips.

"Make it quick," she says.

I wait until she's gone back in the kitchen and then ask hopefully, "Is it you?"

"Cam? It's me, Nina."

"Oh." Something flits around my brain, like a moth getting close to a light. It's not a voice this time, but my own thought: You might be a fool to have all this hope. But it quickly flutters away.

"I need your help."

"Help?" I say. "With what?"

"I'm not feeling so well. I'm a little down. My mom called."

"What did she say?"

"She's not coming back for another week."

"But that's good, isn't it? She won't be bugging you."

"I guess." There's a sadness in Nina's voice. "It's just that . . . I don't know. I'm sorry to bother you, but it's awfully lonely here." When I don't say anything, she adds, "I heard they had to put Griffin in the hospital. He was out on his roof, barking like a dog."

"Who told you that?" I say.

"Nobody. I made it up."

"Aren't you worried about him?"

"Griffin? No. He can take care of himself. Besides, he's always trying to look at my boobs."

"Are you going to school today?" I ask.

"I don't think I am."

"I told you school's not fun when you're not there."

"Well, maybe you could come visit me," she says.

\#

At school, Mrs. Owens tells the class that Griffin won't be with us for a while. It doesn't seem fair about poor Griffin. He can't help it. None of us can.

"It isn't my fault," I say out loud.

"I've never thought that it is," says Mrs. Owens.

I can't believe it and plunge ahead. There is no arm, no voices to keep me from saying my piece. "Stop looking at me that way," I tell her. "You're looking at me as if it were my fault. As if I made him go off."

Attaboy.

"Cameron," warns Mrs. Owens.

"You are," I persist.

You could be the king of this class.

"Cameron, could I see you out in the hall?" She starts walking toward the door.

What's the magic word, Teach?

I wait until she stops and raises her eyebrows at me before I say, "What's the magic word?"

A mousy gasp sweeps the room, and Amy gets ready to drop to the floor.

Mrs. Owens places one hand on her hip. "Please, Cameron," she says.

The room is quiet as I stand and slide back the chair with my heel. I can't help myself and kiss two fingers of one hand as I pass Nina's empty desk. I tap the fingers on top of it.

Asserting oneself is one thing. Acting out aggressively is another.

In the hall, Mrs. Owens possesses me with her eyes. "Are you all right, Cam?" she asks. "This behavior is so unlike you."

Control is essential at a time like this.

"Shut up!"

"Cameron," says Mrs. Owens. "I will not have you talking to me this way."

"Are you going to do to me what you did to Griffin?" I ask.

"What do you think I did to Griffin?"

He's not here.

"He's not here, is he?"

"You know I can't really talk to you about other students, but we all know that some students have a more difficult time than others. Wouldn't you agree with that?"

"Did you ban him from coming back to class?" I ask.

Oh, this is good. See how easy it is? You've got control of her now. See her dance?

"I would never do any such thing," she says. "I am a firm believer in learning for everyone. Banning an individual from that opportunity would go against my beliefs."

"Do you believe sick people can ever get well?"

Mrs. Owens clears her throat and stares straight at me. "Cameron, I'm worried about you. These kinds of questions are so unlike —"

"You don't think people can change."

"Maybe," she says, clearly disturbed, "maybe you and I should go down to the nurse's office."

"No," I say.

"Cameron."

"No." I back up a step. "The law says I don't have to go to the nurse's if I don't want to."

"The law? Cameron, I'm just talking to you one person to another."

I feel penned in by her words. My stomach contracts into a fist. I need to hang on.

"Cameron?"

"Don't touch me," I say, nearly panting. "I need to go to the bathroom." She steps aside as I head down the hall.

"I'll tell the class we'll be a moment," she says as I duck in the boys' room.

But I stay only a second. Soon, I poke my head out the door and see that she's gone back in. I feel a surge as I bolt from the bathroom and down the hall toward the front of the school.

In seconds, I'm outside in the parking lot. I figure I have just a few minutes before they start looking for me, so I head across the street against the light.

I end up at the corner market. A woman is at one of the pumps, swiping her credit card. I watch her while she pumps gas. I can hear clearly the click-click-click as she tops off the tank.

I go inside and buy a Snickers bar and a bag of gummy bears. I pay and walk toward Nina's house.

It starts to rain, and I have to pull my shirt up over my head to keep my hair from getting wet. I sprint the last few yards to get under her carport. Even though I feel shivery, I pull my shirt the rest of the way over my head and hold it, dripping, in my hand. The air circles around me, makes me feel strong.

I don't mess around; I push on the unlocked door. The kitchen is in worse shape than it was the first time I was there. More dishes are stacked in the sink. Little tumbleweeds of hairy dust litter the floor. The cat snoozes in a blue plastic basket half full of dirty clothes. It opens one eye and meows.

"Nina?" I say. I set down the bag of snacks and my shirt but don't stay long in the kitchen. I walk straight to where I found her before and see her on the bed again.

This time I put a knee on the bed and grab her foot, shaking it. "Nina?"

No jumping up and screaming this time. As I watch, one of her eyes pops open and focuses on me. "Took you long enough," she whispers.

"You okay?"

"No," she quickly replies. "But what else is new?" She raises herself up, and I can see that she has her clothes on. She notices me gawking and says, "I saw you coming."

I watch her get out of the bed. She runs both hands through her hair and then stretches.

"Mrs. Owens had me out in the hall and wanted me to go see Mrs. Roosevelt."

"Why?"

"Because I'm independent now and she can't handle it."

"So you ran away from school? And no shirt? Wow, Cam." She puts her hand on my chest, drums her fingers, and then plays with her hair again. I feel goose bumps all over my body.

"It's what happens when you take control of your life," I say.

"What does your mom think?"

"She doesn't like it. But she has to live with it because it's the law." I narrow my eyes. "I thought you were depressed today," I say.

"I was until I saw you."

A shiver goes through my body and takes a place very near my heart. "You mean that?"

She nods and stretches again, then plops down on the end of the bed. I look at her bare feet, then hear:

Hello, Cam.

"Oh, hello." At last.

I love you.

"I love you so much," I say without thinking. It's

real and so automatic. Then I wake up to the voice. "You don't know how much," I add.

Nina bunches up her face. "Really?"

I've missed you.

I feel my body hum. "Oh, I've missed you too."

"How cool," says Nina.

"I can't get you out of my mind."

Nina turns into something different. She stretches out her legs, and they're like beasts. Her toes curl and uncurl, her head bends to the side. Crisp red spots dot her cheeks. "I'm so surprised," she says.

I was so worried I'd never speak to you again. I know there is no greater love than what you and I have. I've been waiting so long to talk to you again.

"Let's talk, then," I say. "I've been waiting too."

I spiral down to the floor and lean against Nina's bookcase. I no longer feel a chill. I hold my knees and press my bare chest against them. I'm so happy, I feel like crying.

"What should we talk about?" Nina says.

"What?"

"I said what do you want to talk about?"

You're just the boy I need. I get so lonely, Cam. And there's no one else I can talk to the way I can talk to you.

"Okay. Let's talk about anything we want to. I'm not going anywhere. I don't want to lose you again."

Nina smiles as if she were made of sugar. "I didn't know you felt this way," she says. "I mean, I hoped you felt this way, but I wasn't sure, and I didn't want to push it."

She leans in closer to me. My eyes finally focus on her but then briefly turn inward before they clear again. "And I'll try so hard not to scare you off," she says. "I promise."

I close my eyes and my lips pucker just the slightest. I suddenly feel another presence; something is getting closer. I can sense warmth next to my lips.

Uh, wake up, Cammy, you don't want to miss this.

"Be quiet," I whisper.

Knock, knock, fool. Your manhood is waiting.

I blast open my eyes and there is Nina, her face so close, I see her everywhere. I feel her lips against mine. It makes my head whirl with pleasure.

"I guess that was pretty good, huh?" she says, leaning back.

I close my eyes again.

Where were we?

"We have all the time in the world," I say. "You and I forever."

"Do you think anyone else feels this way?" Nina says.

"No one," I say. "There's nobody else in the world."

seventeen

IT'S easy to slip onto the bus after school. Nina and I both wait across the road until the line of buses starts coming, and we use them to shield ourselves. While we wait for the door to open, we concoct a plan. It's good, but complicated and maybe hard to put into action. Nina waits for me to get on and then cocks her head as I leave. I feel ecstatic because The Girl is in my life again.

Beth is in the back with a couple of her friends. When the bus starts moving, she quickly sneaks up and sits next to me. "Why is your teacher looking for you?" she says.

"I don't know. Ask her."

"The vice principal called me today and wanted to know if I'd seen you."

"What do those freaks care, anyway?" I say, folding my arms at my chest.

"Mom called too. I had to talk pretty fast to keep her from getting hold of the sheriff. I guess you can't go back to school until you have some meeting with them."

"I wish they'd just leave me alone," I say.

"They will. Once you do exactly as they say. Look at me. They don't even ask me about Dylan anymore. They think I'm being so obedient."

"I don't want to do exactly what they want," I say. But a bit of thunder unloads in the back of my head, and I steel myself for the inevitable.

That's the spirit, boy.

Beth frowns but scoots to the back of the bus. When I turn to look, she's jabbering with her friends again.

Someone at the school must have seen me get on the bus, because Mom is waiting in her car at the stop. I can see her through the windshield; her lips are set in a line and her eyes are just staring. When Beth and I get off, Mom jumps out of the car and tries to block our way.

The bus hisses off and Beth starts walking, but Mom and I just stand there like gunfighters, only I don't feel like drawing first.

"Wasn't the last time enough?" she says. "Wasn't it

bad enough for us all? I can't believe you're doing this to me again. Where were you?"

But now I feel loose and free and walk around her. I don't even turn around when I hear her get in the car and start it up. Pretty soon, it creeps along behind me, crunching the gravel. For a second, I think she'd rather run me down and be done with it, and that makes me sneak a peek. But she's got her window rolled down and her arm out as she eases along.

"We can make this easier if you just get in," she says.

"No," I say, and realize I never knew how blessed a word it was before. I calculate how long it would take me to catch up to Beth, but she's in hyperdrive and I'm starting to sweat.

"Cameron, even Dr. Simons says it's better if we talk."

Too much talk and not enough action. You need this, boy. See how it worked with your teacher? You need to take your stand. Do what I say and it will all work out.

I keep staring ahead, but I can't resist saying, "You don't really want to talk; you only want to order me around."

"Cam, that's not true. I'm only interested in what's best for you." When I don't say anything, she says, "Cam? Cam? Do you want me to call the authorities to come get you?"

After a second, the engine revs up and I hear some gravel shoot out from the tires. Pretty soon, Mom is moving up beside me.

"Cam? Talk to me."

"I'm not crazy," I shout, scaring even myself. "Stop acting like I am. I'm just mad."

She guns it again and the car jerks ahead. About ten yards in front of me, she veers it to the left and cuts me off. I think she expects me to walk right up to the passenger door and get in. Meanwhile, up ahead, Beth stops and watches us.

"You're more than just mad," Mom says.

Keep walking.

It's as if the car weren't even there. It's a little tricky with the backpack on, but I step on the bumper and lift myself up onto her hood. It bends and moans as I step across it and then jump down. Beth laughs and claps.

I expect to hear the car as I start walking again, but it's quiet back there. After another ten yards, I turn and see my mom with her head on her hand clutching the window well. I think if she'd just give up, it would all be easier. I walk carefully the rest of the way home.

#

We have a family meeting after Dad gets home. Even he doesn't get to eat until we're done, and that makes him grumpy because we have our meeting at the kitchen table and he wrinkles his nose, sniffing for dinner.

Mom is very democratic. She even lets Beth speak her mind, and Beth says, "Why do I have to be involved in this stupid meeting?"

"Because we're a family," Mom says. "Isn't that right, Dad?"

Dad nods and starts picking at a callus on his thumb.

"Well, I officially think it's stupid," says Beth. "Cam should be able to do what he wants."

"Okay," says Mom. "Maybe I should state the problem first." She folds her hands and rests them on top of the table. Her fingers look like a pile of bleached-out little wieners. "I think that we have a serious situation in the family, and I'd like to address it. Even though we all know what the situation is, I'll spell it out. One of us, Cameron, has a dangerous condition that he is making worse by not doing the responsible thing. In layman's terms, he needs to take medication, and he's probably not doing it. This makes his condition worse. Today, Cameron chose to run away from school and was nowhere to be found, and I personally think it's a result of his not taking the medication and ignoring his serious condition."

"I didn't run away from school," I said.

"Well, then, what —"

"I was checking to see if a friend was okay."

"What friend?" Mom asks.

"That's none of your business."

"Cam," Dad warns.

Careful now. Play it smart.

I can tell Mom wants to say something really mean, such as spilling the secret of when she caught me talking to The Girl in the rain, but she bites her lip. "Cameron, are we talking about that imaginary girlfriend of yours?"

Is this respect?

I shake my head. "I'm not saying anything more."

"Because if we are, then we're not going to get anywhere."

"It looks like this is all about Cam," Beth says. "Can I be excused?"

"Keep quiet," Dad says, and he gives Beth his military look. He then turns to me. "Cam, from now on I want you to treat your mom with respect. And that goes for you, too, Beth. I've had enough of this sarcastic crap from the two of you."

"It's Mom's fault," Beth tries, but Dad holds up a hand.

"If you can give your friends respect, then you can give it to your own mother as well."

It's quiet for a few seconds, but I can hear Beth's

brain working. I can't stand this sort of quiet, so I say, "It was someone else."

"You can't just take off from school," Dad says.

Yes, you can. You did.

"And are you taking your meds or not?" he asks.

"I am," I say softly. But even I can hear the little question mark at the end, and I can see that Mom doesn't believe me. She folds her arms at her chest. I hold my hands out in front of me. It's risky, but right now they're perfectly calm. "Do these look like the hands of a crazy person?"

"Please don't use that word," she says.

My father stares at my hands, but it doesn't seem to matter to him. "Taking off like that just makes everybody worry about you," he says.

You don't need to be worried about me. Everything's just fine.

"I don't need to be worried about," I say.

"As long as you live here with us, we reserve the right to worry about you," Dad says.

Beth mumbles something that I can't understand, but Dad has had enough. He stands up, towering over the rest of us. "I didn't want to have to go this far with it, but you've forced my hand."

He looks sternly at me. "Starting tomorrow, Cam,

you will go to the doctor and get a shot. And you'll get one every week until it's all cleared up."

"Dad. No. It's the law."

"If you think you're big enough to deal with the law, then go right ahead. You want to sue me for caring about you? I'd like to see that one."

I'll do it.

"No," I say. I'm talking to The Other Guy, but Dad thinks I'm on him.

He wags a big finger at both Beth and me. "Listen closely, you two. You've got a week to shape up. That's right, a week. I'm going to be watching you, and your mother is going to be reporting to me. If things haven't changed in your attitude, then I'm laying down some additional rules, and you probably won't like them, either."

"But you can't—"

"Try me," he shouts. "Just try me." Then he turns to Beth. "And if you expect to ever see your friends again, you'd better shape up yourself."

Beth's eyes glow like a werewolf's, but she quickly stares down at the table.

"Understood?" Dad asks.

"Understood," Mom says. She smirks and I want to tell her off.

But I don't, and Beth whispers, "Understood," while in my head I hear:

Oh yeah. Understood all right.

#

Up in my room, I'm making a decision. In or out? Am I in this family or am I out? I realize it is one of those decisions that can make your brain tip out of balance, but somehow, after Dad's ultimatum at the dinner table, it doesn't matter all that much. And I'm already out of balance anyway.

I'm in the middle of my plan when Beth knocks on my door.

"No," I say, but she comes in anyway.

She takes one look at me and says, "I thought you were up to something." On the bed, my coat and my watch cap are waiting for me to put them on.

"You should be too," I say. I position the watch cap on my head.

"Where are you going?" Beth asks.

"Out," I say. I busy myself putting underwear and socks in my coat pocket. Then I think it's stupid and pull them out.

"Uh, this might not be the best time to go out," she says.

"You heard him," I say, stopping in the middle of

the floor. "I have one day. Then my life as I know it ends."

Beth licks her lips and says, "She's right, isn't she? You're not taking your meds."

"Who cares?" I say.

"Are you okay?"

"Course I'm okay."

"Look, Cam," she says. "I'm pissed off too, but I don't think it's a good idea to run away from home."

"Who's running away?" I ask. "I'm just going down to the door and stepping out. I don't plan to run."

She grabs at my chin and forces me to look in her eyes. "You're not okay, Cam. I can see it."

"It's not your life," I say.

"But where are you going?" Beth asks again.

I shrug, but I do know.

"To your girlfriend's?" she asks.

I can't tell if she's making fun of me or not, but I nod anyway. I expect her to say something that Mom would, but she doesn't.

"Be careful" is all she says.

eighteen

IT is easy to leave home after a fight. Mom, Dad, and Beth are someplace else in the house licking their wounds and figuring out whether they won or not. I know Mom and Dad are sure they're the winners. It's time to prove them wrong. So, arming my hands through the sleeves of my jacket and carrying Mom's little flashlight, I turn the knob quietly and I'm out the back door.

It's dark, and the breeze is cool enough to make me shiver and strong enough to rattle the new leaves of the vine maples as I make my way down the driveway. It looks like the breeze might have blown the rain away. When I go down around the corner, I snap on the flashlight.

It doesn't take long to get to the highway, not as long as on the foot-dragging school mornings. Once I get there, I'm not sure what my next move will be. I stand by the mailbox while a couple of cars whiz by. Neither of them slows, but the last one throws up a spray of muddy water that coats my shoes.

Last chance to make the right decision. Slow and steady wins the race.

"Do you even know what you're talking about?" But what The Professor says does make me balk for a moment. A new life seems a long way off right about now.

Are you giving up on me?

"No."

You're not paying attention the way you used to. It's The Girl, isn't it?

We can do it. The two of us together can. We can have whatever we want because we have love.

"Is that really all it takes?" I say.

Just look at your parents. Aren't they in love?

"Well yeah. They are in love."

And they've been together all this time. What do you think has held them together?

And that's all it takes. Of course it's their love and having each other to rely on. That's what I want. Without people wondering whether I can handle it or not.

I cross the road and take off walking. It's a lot different from riding the school bus, more at ground level, like Dylan's car. Blinding headlights come toward me and from behind, where I am sure I make a silhouette. I walk into Lexington, which is about a mile through and through, and an hour after that, I'm under the railroad bridge.

To get to Nina's place, I would have to walk another four miles into town, cross on the Peter Crawford Bridge, and then backtrack to a point that I can almost see now just across the river. But there is a shorter way, and I'd thought about it a few times while on the bus. The local railroad crosses the river right where I am now standing. A car comes along, and its headlights flash higher on the bridge where I can just make out the familiar words in big red lettering:

DANGER! LOG TRAIN OVERHEAD!

It used to scare me when the train would go over just when the bus was going under, and I thought the logs might fall off and crush us all.

Strangely, I'm not scared now. But I don't want to be caught, so I jump down in the ditch when another car's headlights show in the distance. The tall wet grass soaks my pants. When the car goes by, it's another easy decision. I carefully remove my jacket and tie it around my neck. Now my arms have more freedom. I shine the light up the huge Lincoln Log timbers of the railroad bridge. It's as if the structure were made for me. I notice that the ends of the timbers might just jut out at the right proportions for me to climb all the way to the top. I reach up and feel a timber. It smells like creosote.

But before I start, I hear from The Professor:

The local log train does a night run. The chances of crossing the bridge on foot and making it out alive are 50 percent. You must think about this.

"But it's way shorter," I say.

Yes; however, it's a long way down.

Before The Professor can say another word, a second voice roars in:

Do it anyway.

Hard and demanding. As if I must obey or else.

Do it now, chicken boy.

Anxiety courses through me. I grab on to a timber.

"Back off a little," I say.

Cock-a-doodle-doo!

I heft myself up, worrying as my jacket swings out. It is surprisingly easy to hoist myself to the next timber, and the next.

That's it, boy. That's it. Could've done it all along.

The Other Guy is right. What had been keeping me from doing something like this? Maybe I always should have listened to him. Now, instead of fear, I feel a pulse of courage and scramble even faster up toward the dark top. I can smell the mill up here, the trees, the dankness of the river below.

My heart goes out to you, Cameron, and I certainly understand your motives, but is this really the way to go?

"I like you better when you just give me the facts."

Sweat breaks out on my face but is quickly lapped up by the breeze. I stop to jam the flashlight between my front teeth. Now I can look up and see the next timber more easily.

It takes me fifteen more minutes to get to the top. Meanwhile, the headlights below get dimmer and dimmer. The wind dies down as a light fog drifts around me. Above it, the moon momentarily wins a battle with the clouds. It shines on the slick silvery rails. I reach up and put all my weight onto one of those rails. As I lift myself up and around the last timber, I lose my grip and hold on by only one hand. I think the slipperiness will make my hand slide off, but it holds for an instant, long enough for me to wrap my entire arm around the timber and secure myself. From there, I slowly drag my body up onto the top.

I gently untie the arms of my jacket and lay it on my chest as I rest on my back. My breath comes quickly, but it feels good.

Hello, Cam.

"I hear you," I say.

I never knew you were so strong.

"I don't care what The Other Guy says. I am a man."

My man.

Lying there, I know I could listen to her voice forever.

You left home. You ran. That takes a lot of guts. You're really in charge of yourself now, aren't you? In charge of us both. It makes me want you even more.

I stand up then and put on my jacket. I feel I might be able to take care of the whole world. At this point on the bridge I'm still a few feet from the edge of the river. It runs slow and smelly way below me. I take off toward the other side. In a few steps, I start to see the moon's reflection off the surface between the timbers. I wonder how brave I must look from down below. I wonder what my mother would think if she happened to see me. The boy she so carefully protected is now in the worst possible place she could think of.

In fact, nobody would think I could do this. If kids in the regular classes saw me now, they would start talking about me differently. They might even step back when I come down the hall. I'd hear whispers all around me. "He's the one. He's the guy who walked the bridge at night."

Damn straight.

I could go in through the regular school door.

And I'm going to get you through that door, big guy.

"You and I," I say.

The walking is uneven. It's just wide enough so that I have to stretch my step a little. I can't get too comfortable, or I might find myself shooting down through the timbers, bouncing off them like a pinball, and then splashing into the water, unconscious, drifting down to the Columbia and out to sea, never to be heard from again. How would my mom feel then?

I stop in the middle. I think I hear a distant whistle, but maybe it's just my nerves. I wait another few seconds, hear nothing, and then take off again. When the clouds take back the sky and the moon fades, it grows darker, harder to see. I wave my flashlight into the blackness, but then pull it back sharply. What if someone can see me, even from way over on the hills? What if they call the cops and they come to get me? Who knows, they're probably already out looking for me. Thwarted before I even get started. I snap out the light and wait a moment until my eyes have adjusted.

I trip once and cast out wildly for a hold but realize there isn't one. I fall and hit the hard timbers. My foot hangs between two of them. I can feel my heart zinging in my chest. So this is what it's like. This is what those mountain climbers feel. This is what runners feel before a race. It must be. All bad and good and exciting at the same time. I let my legs dangle awhile.

"I love this!" I shout.

I'm getting a little worried, Cameron.

"I don't need you," I say. "I can do this on my own." And to prove it, I stand up again and start walking.

Kind of like the life you want, isn't it?

In order to make it in the world, you must proceed with caution. There is happiness in caution.

I wonder if The Professor has ever given me the right advice. It seems that in order to make it in The Professor's world, you have to deny yourself. What if there's a world where all you have to do is trust yourself? You just have to know that when you stick your foot out, it's going to hit the next timber. You shouldn't even have to look down.

Well, theoretically speaking. Which means the bridge wasn't built with exact measurements between the ties. I'm sure the plans started out that way, but they didn't take into account human error. About three-quarters of the way across I am looking up through the hazy clouds and take the wrong step. The front of my shoe slips against the tie and I almost fall through. Almost. But I am lucky and catch myself before I do.

Ah, Cameron. Now it's more than 50 percent. More than a 50 percent chance of failure the longer you're caught between the ties.

I like the way you challenge yourself, Cam. It means you aren't just going to sit back and watch life pass you by.

"Thank you," I say. But I can see I've got myself into quite a challenge. Although I can barely feel a narrow support somewhere beneath me, I don't know if it will hold my entire weight. I feel like a prairie dog, with only my head and shoulders poking out above the level of the rails. And although there's no danger of my really falling because of the grip I have, I'm going to have a tough time boosting myself up enough to climb back onto the bridge. And this time, before I can think of any other problem I've gotten myself into, I do hear a faint whistle.

Hey now. Here we go. Time to prove yourself.

I suddenly have to pee. Jamming the flashlight back in my mouth, I brace both hands on the creosoted ties and try to lift my lower body up like a gymnast on the rings. In a few seconds, my arms are shaking badly and the strength is leaking out of my muscles. I gently ease myself back on my elbows.

Uh, oh-oh.

"I can figure this out."

Cam. Isn't that the train?

"I think so."

You'll get us out, of course.

"We're together now, aren't we? Of course I'll get us out." But I'm not so sure. After a few seconds of rest, I try to leverage myself up again. I get a little higher than before, but my muscles are even shakier this time. Meanwhile, the sound of the train whistle comes definitely closer.

I couldn't have planned this better if I'd tried.

"A little less sarcasm," I say. "And a little more help."

I look around me. There is nothing to grab on to, to help hoist myself up. I crush against the timber and try to boost my body, using the the wood as a lever. But I'm not going anywhere.

Cam?

"I'm trying," I say. "I'll think of something."

It's coming. I can sense it.

And she's right. I can feel a rumbling in the timbers. A thundering herd is about to round the corner up ahead. I desperately try to recall how much space is below log cars. Will there be enough room?

If we die, I will always remember this happy life I've had with you.

"We're not going to die," I say, just as the heavy beam of the engine light shines against the timbers. It is loud now, its warning precise. I no longer have to pee. In fact, everything is blocked in my body.

Cam? Cameron? I'm getting a little worried.

I wonder now what it is I can do. It looks like death is barreling along toward me. And I definitely don't want this.

`I'm so sorry, Cameron.`

There's too much to think about, too much to say. I want to tell Beth I'm sorry if I've embarrassed her by being her crazy little brother. I want to tell Dad that I wish I could have been more of what he wanted me to be. And I want to tell Mom that it's not her fault.

The end is the end is the end is the end.

These words do not comfort me as the engine comes around the curve and straightens its light so I am full on washed in it. I close my eyes, but I can still see the bright light behind my lids. I feel a strong wind blow into my face. I wince and prepare for the worst.

nineteen

IT is natural to hunker down before a big blow comes,
and this is what I do. I squeeze myself between the timbers, balancing on some unseen narrow wooden support. But the broad sweep of the engine's power nearly
knocks me over and down through the space. I can hear
everything, feel almost nothing. At times I think the
grabbing wind will suck the air out of my lungs, and I
gasp as if it has.

It takes maybe five minutes for it to go over, but it
is the longest five minutes of my life. Once I know my
head isn't going to be chopped off, I get used to being
beneath the train. I try to look up to the undercarriage
of the cars, but they are going too fast and all I see is a

dusty blur. My arms start to shake and I fight to keep them steady.

It is so noisy and windy that it takes me a moment to realize the train has finally passed over me. I peek up over the timber and see the red light of the last car disappear around the bend.

I love the roller coaster.

"You do, huh?"

Yes. It's thrilling. When you feel the thrill in your stomach and you just have to scream it out.

I don't really want to chat. Instead, I try to figure out a way to get up and off the bridge. I know there are other trains that will be coming along, and I don't want to end up like that panicked prairie dog, just popping up and down out of my hole whenever danger is close.

I try the flashlight again and in a moment see the way. It has been there all along. Where my legs dangle, I see a ladder connected timber to timber all the way across the rest of the bridge. If I swing my legs, I can catch it and crawl to safety.

And there is even better news. After about five timbers' worth of crawling, the ladder connects to another one, which I take up onto the surface of the bridge. I lie there to catch my breath. No voices, but a certain amount of real satisfaction. It doesn't last, though. The electric shock is back in my legs. In a moment, I get up and trot to the other side.

#

At the end, I jump off the bridge and slide along the rocky ballast until I hit solid ground. I know my way from here, and after a half hour of picking through old train tracks and gravel roads, I stand in front of Nina's house. The porch light throws a weak semicircle onto the lawn, but I can make out another light in the kitchen. I go to the front door and knock.

I see the curtain rustle, hear a slight scream, and, in seconds, Nina pulls the door open.

"I didn't think you would come so soon," she says, yanking me in. The first thing I notice is how warm and clean everything is. I can see into the kitchen; every dish is drying on the plastic rack. It smells of pine cleaner. I take in a big breath.

"I've been at it all afternoon," she says. She comes toward me with her lips puckered, and I quickly turn my cheek before she plants a big one right below my eye. "So this is your game," she says.

In spite of her chipper attitude, I can see dark half-moons below her eyes. I want to tell her about the bridge, but it suddenly feels like a very private thing. So

I just tell her about the family meeting and how hard it was to find a way out of the house.

"They're going to keep a closer watch on you?" she says.

"Not anymore," I say.

"Ooh, there's my new Cameron guy."

"You'd better get used to him because I think he's here to stay."

She walks over to a wobbly sofa with an afghan covering the back. Plopping down, she asks, "So how many days is it for you?"

"I've lost count," I say. "And I don't care anymore. What about you?"

She shrugs. "I don't really know. A long time. Long enough to be almost done throwing up and feeling like my head's about to explode."

"What's that about?"

"Side effects. They don't always tell you that part. You can get hooked, and when you go off, all kinds of weird things happen."

I don't want to hear about any side effects. "So are we just going to hang out here?" I say.

"I don't know where else we can go. Even if Mom does come back eventually, she won't stay and she won't care if you're here."

I finally walk over and sit down next to her. I play

with loose yarn on the afghan. "My parents are going to know I'm gone tonight. They probably know already. And they're the kind who will come looking."

"Do they know about me?"

"Not really," I say. "I told my mom I had a girlfriend, but I didn't tell her the name."

"*The* name or my name?"

When I turn to see what she means, I see a hurt look on her face. "I didn't tell them any name," I say.

We won't, of course, go to school, especially since Nina said the school officials had gotten tired of checking in on her when she was absent because her mother would never cooperate with them. But for me, I know school will be the first place my mother will look when she can't find me at home.

We decide that I will sleep in Nina's mom's room. While my parents' room is kind of old-fashioned and modern at the same time, this room is like a bad dream. A double bed just about fills the whole thing, and on top of it rests a shiny deep purple bedspread with little rips along the seams. It is one of those beds with shelves in the headboard, and I find old *National Geographics,* a red Bible, and a photo of what looks like Nina's mom driving a bumper car at a fair.

On another shelf, a ceramic chipmunk sits on a

ceramic throne dotted with fake jewels. Next to it is a plaster hand cast that Nina must have made at school when she was young. One of the fingers is missing. The room smells like a combination of cigarettes, pine cleaner, and mildew. The cat pads in and jumps on the end of the bed, twitching its tail.

Nina comes up behind me. "I changed the sheets," she says. "They were starting to crawl on their own."

"It'll do," I say, then rethink it. "I appreciate it."

I get into bed and turn out the light about midnight. But there is a strange glow creeping in from the kitchen, and I get up to check it out. It's on the stove and is flickering ever so slightly. I search for a few seconds to find a switch I can turn it off with but have no luck. I check back to Nina's room, but her door is closed and I can't see anything. I go back to mine and shut the door behind me.

I try to sleep, but my head is buzzing too much. I can't get my parents out of my head. My dad is probably calming down my mom, but she will be crying and trying to think of a place they haven't looked. I don't want to put them through this, but it can't be helped.

I have done something, I think. I have done what everybody said I couldn't do. I have made a decision and followed through with it. I have done something that is for my own good. And it hasn't hurt me, has it?

I check myself out. The buzz is still there in the back of my brain, but as long as it stays the way it is, I'll be all right. My body is a little shaky, and I feel like I'm sort of in another world, but I actually am at Nina's house. The voices are quiet right now. It looks like I have control over them too.

I take a deep breath and think, Dr. Simons, I hope you're right. Maybe all the bad will disappear on its own. I lie quietly on the pillow. Maybe I can be normal after all.

I wake up to a familiar smell and at first I think I'm at home in my own bed, but all the angles are wrong. It's as if I'm upside down or sideways. I was too excited to sleep much, finally getting a few hours before morning. I raise myself up and the smell gets stronger. Eggs. I close my eyes and can hear them frying.

I roll out of bed and pull on my pants. When I open the door, I can see into the kitchen. Nina is standing at the stove, wearing an apron over a pink terry-cloth robe with loose strings sprouting out all over it. She holds a spatula in one hand and pokes at the eggs. I come up behind her just in time for her to whirl around, hand me the spatula, and run into the bathroom.

"Watch those," she says over her shoulder.

When she comes back out, she's as pale as a ghost.

It makes the dark circles under her eyes even darker. She takes the spatula from me.

"Morning sickness," she says.

"What?"

"Sorry. Bad joke. It's the pills. As I said, I'm still a little sick once in a while." She moves the eggs over to the side of the skillet, but it's too late; they're all crispy on the edges.

"Don't worry," I say, anticipating her. "I like them that way."

But she shakes her head and turns the flame off. "I'm no good at this," she says.

I pick up the spatula and scrape it under one of the eggs. I hold it up over the pan as oil drips through the slats.

"Maybe the cat will eat them," she says.

"I'm sure they're great," I say. And to prove it, I reach over and with my teeth, pull the egg to the edge of the spatula and bite into it. It's hard and salty, but I chew it, smiling. I swallow and nod.

"Oh, you're just saying that," she says. But I can tell she is pleased. "The problem is, we don't have anything else to eat here, and we probably shouldn't be out in public."

Then I remember and go into the living room. I

grab the remote and snap on the TV. I get a whole lot of snow and a barely detectable image of a person.

"They shut off the cable a long time ago," Nina says. "And the stupid antenna her old boyfriend rigged up blew to pieces on the roof during the last storm. Sorry."

"It's better if I don't see them looking for me," I say. "It'll only make it worse."

"So what do you want to do?" she asks, swinging her arms back and forth.

"I don't know. What do you want to do?"

We stand staring at each other and I wonder what I've done.

Hello, Cam. Are you bored?

There's a shivery smile in my words. "Yes, a little."

"What?" says Nina.

Tell her you've got to eat.

"I've got to eat," I say.

I need you healthy and strong. A giggle from The Girl, and I think I get it.

I laugh and see worry bloom on Nina's face. "Cameron?"

"It's okay. It's just that I think we should eat something."

"Those were the last of the eggs."

A human being can last approximately

eighteen days without food. Much less without water. A corpse, of course, does not have to worry about food and water. I have a suggestion, Cameron. Go back home. And what's all this giggling about?

"Wrong," I say.

Just a suggestion.

"I have a few bucks," I say. "Do you want to go to the store?"

"I have some too," Nina says. "I'll go, but I don't think it's a good idea for you to go with me. Somebody'll recognize you."

"Because I'm so popular?" I say.

"No. Because you're the only one with somebody who cares about you."

While Nina scoops up the money her mother left on the table, I dig into my pocket and pull out ten dollars and some change. I hand it over to her. "Get some protein," I say.

#

After Nina leaves, I go back into the bedroom and lie down on the bed.

She's gone, Cam.

"I know."

That means we're alone.

"I thought that's why you were giggling." I am trembling and sit up further. It's the joy in her voice that sets me off. It feels so honest and real. While I'm lying against the headboard, something twists my hair and I turn quickly to see what's there. Just the ceramic chipmunk. But I hear giggling again and lean back against the bed.

"What's going on?" I say.

The noise stops, and immediately I feel something faintly touching the top of my shoulder. This time I roll over and jump out of bed. "Who is it?" I say. "Who's doing that?"

Silly boy. Who do you think?

Now I'm completely baffled. "How is it possible?" I say.

What's real, Cam?

I can't believe I'm saying this, but she may be right. Reality is perception, Mr. Galloway. How one sees the world is one's own reality.

"I told you I don't need you," I say.

And there it is again. A slight touch on my arm, like real fingers traveling down to my wrist. It jumps from my arm to my stomach and rubs me there. Then it moves back up across my chest to my neck, where the fingers gently caress the hollow.

"Is that you?" My voice now sounds huskier.

Yes, Cam. It's me.

The touch fades and I reach out, searching for her hand. But I end up grasping only at air. "I want you," I say.

I'm right here, Cam.

But trying to get hold of her only frustrates me more. Like a blind person, my arms are out in front of me, sweeping back and forth. Her giggle floats around my head. "How do I do this?" I cry.

Hold still.

I stop all the flailing. My arms stick out in front of me, ready to hold her.

Pucker up.

And I do. I squinch my lips together. I am so excited now; I have never felt anything like this. And it is at this moment that Nina comes into the room.

She throws a plastic bag on the bed and says, "What are you doing?"

I open my eyes, my arms still extended. I notice how empty the room is. "Uh . . ."

"You're with her, aren't you?" Nina says.

When I don't answer, she grabs the bag and runs out of the room. I hear her door slam.

I finally bring down my arms and wrap them around myself.

The coast is clear.

But the moment is over and I feel betrayed. Instead of speaking, I just shake my head.

You don't want to anymore?

"No," I say.

There is a pause. I think I hear Nina in her room. She could be crying.

What now?

"I'm a little confused."

Maybe I can help you.

"I feel lost sometimes. As if I don't know what to do."

Don't worry. You're not lost. I still have you up in my brain.

"In your brain?" I laugh.

I'm serious.

"It's just a weird thing for you to say."

She is quiet and I feel fidgety once more.

"You said that I'm still in your brain. *Your* brain."

I know what I said. But what's so funny?

"But you're in *my* brain. How could I be in yours?"

Oh that's cute. You think I'm . . .

"What?"

The truth is, Cameron, there's a lot you don't know about me.

And then a pulse of fear shoots through my gut. I instantly feel all turned around. I slide off the edge of the bed. "I need something to do," I say out loud.

twenty

WORRY has entered my body. What else don't I know? If I'm in her brain . . . I shake my head. The whole idea scares me, and I look harder for something to do. I latch on to the television situation.

I go out in the tiny backyard and look up at the roof. Right at the chimney, there is a loosely attached antenna. It starts out straight at the bottom, but about halfway up, it bends at a forty-five-degree angle as if a monster wind hit it straight on. A brown ribbon of wire flows down the side of the house from it and then in through a hole cut in the window sash.

I'm not allowed on the roof at home, but this is not home, so I go searching in the carport and find what I'm looking for hanging off a pair of spikes on one of the beams. I take the ladder down, run it out to the side of the house, and test it. It's a bit wobbly, but I think it will do.

I carefully climb up, stopping for a second in the middle to let it adjust to my weight, and then quickly reach the slick edge of the roof. From there I can see that moss is sprouting in hairy clumps all the way across the surface. Not a good situation for a guy trying to get up to the chimney.

I test the shingles with my hand: they are slippery. Maybe climbing is a bad idea. I remember something Dr. Simons once told me. If you think too much or too long, it can get you into trouble. So I stop thinking and struggle onto the roof, accidentally kicking the ladder as I do, so that it falls with a crash into the rhododendrons. In seconds, the whole front of me is dark from the wet moss. Ahead I see the antenna.

Either you do or you don't fix it. Any bets?

I weather a sense of doom the way I used to when the voices first came and it felt just like this, being out on a ledge with no one around to help and gravity slowly starting to tug me down. I claw at the slimy shingles and manage to dig my hands into them, stopping my downward creep.

Interesting.

I bring my knees up under me, which helps me feel

more secure. Slowly, I crawl up the roof until I make it to the chimney. I grab on to the side and pull myself up to where I'm facing the antenna.

It takes only a few seconds to straighten out the flimsy metal. When I do, I raise up my hands in a victory clasp and make a sound like a crowd cheering. A mistake. I slip on the shingles and fall hard. Again, I'm sliding down, but this time on the other side of the gable. I turn on my stomach and dig into the shingles. Gradually I slow and then stop once more.

I should scream out. I should cry out loud. But instead a different dam breaks inside me, and a torrent of hysterical laughter comes gushing out. The kind you hear on late-night slasher movies. I don't know what makes it happen, but everything seems so funny now. Years of funny. I laugh so hard that I break loose one of the shingles and have to dig again to get a better hold.

Hello, Cam.

Her voice does not shut me up. Every pore seems to bleed laughter.

It's so good to see you this way.

"Crazy fun," I say.

It's the way it should be. Every single day should be crazy fun.

I can't stop. Dancing goose bumps twirl up and down my arms. My stomach hurts from being slammed against the roof. Waves of a strange relief pulse through my body.

Forget what I said before, Cam. It doesn't matter who's in whose brain. I love you just the way you are right now.

"I love you, too," I say, gulping for air. Her voice is so delicate that I can't help myself. It hurts as if I were being squeezed from the inside. I want to hold myself tightly, but if I do, I'll go sliding down the roof.

"Cameron?"

At first I think it's The Girl again, but when I peek down to the lawn, I see Nina standing there.

"What are you doing?" she asks.

"Being stuck," I say.

"How'd you get up there?"

"The ladder. Only it had a little accident."

At first she's tentative, then breaks into a big smile. "It did, did it? You know there's a better way to get up and down, don't you?"

"All I'm thinking of now is getting down," I say.

"Well, there's a place right next to where the carport meets the roof. I'll go climb up there and let you know when you can let go."

"Let go?" I say, but she's already gone.

In a minute I hear her voice behind me. "Now, if you just let yourself slide down to where I am, I'll catch you."

"Uh, you're not that big, Nina. What if I don't stop and we both fall off?"

"Then we both fall off, I guess," she says. I can't see her, but I can tell what kind of look she's giving me.

I can't do it unless I can see my target, so I squirm a little to the side where I can look through the space between my elbow and my body. And there, half of Nina shows above the roofline. She does not look as mad as she did when she first got back from the store. I want to think about this, but it's as if Dr. Simons were there, ripping my fingers from the shingles. One shingle breaks off and I start to slide; another breaks and I'm going faster.

"Straighten out!" Nina yells behind me. "So I can catch your feet!"

But it's a bumpy ride and I can't control myself. Some of the humps of moss are planted deep in the shingles, and when I go over them, they twist and turn me as if I were nothing but a bouncing pinball.

Nina's still yelling, but I can't make out what she says. The hurt on the inside turns into a roller-coaster wave of thrill. The last thing I hear is Nina screaming out, "Cameron!" just as I hit something solid, quiver a moment, and then feel both of us go down in a tumbling, shouting heap.

#

My hands claw at nothing. Somehow, Nina and I disengage, so that when I hit, it is solid earth beneath me.

Whump!

I can't catch my breath even though I try with every muscle I have. It's a bad way to go, and I curse my dumb luck as the world fades around me. But just before it gets completely dark, Nina's face rises over mine.

"Can you believe it?" she shouts. I feel a light spray of spit as she does. "We lived!"

My lips are stuck together, but it's getting lighter.

"What?" she says. She turns and presses her ear against my lips. Then she raises her head. "I might have to do mouth to mouth."

Now I can't tell if I've really gone crazy or she has. Where is the mad girl from a while ago? Again, I try to say something, but my lips are on strike. I try blinking my eyes and I manage to catch Nina's. They are strangely misty and focused. I see her lean down and I feel her lips on mine. She gently blows against them.

Electricity flashes behind my eyes, and one of my legs jumps uncontrollably.

Nina rises again and smiles. I can smell her and she smells good. Leaning back down, she kisses me again, only this time she presses harder. My lips naturally part, and our front teeth clink. Suddenly I suck in a deep, precious breath. It feels like I've stolen it from Nina's lungs. I push her off and sit up.

"Maybe that wasn't the best way down," I say.

Nina is on her back, giggling. Her feet are slamming against the grass.

"What's wrong with you?"

"Nothing," she manages to say, and then starts a laugh riot again. "You should have seen yourself." Seeing her kicking her feet lights a fire in my stomach, and I laugh too.

"I'm alive," I say in a Dr. Frankenstein voice. "I'm alive!"

"Barely," she says as she rolls toward me. I feel the wet grass and realize that I am a shivering mess. Nina's lips are blue, and the bottom one quivers as I pause to study it. It looks like the most beautiful piece of skin I've ever seen.

"You're not half bad looking," I say, and instantly cough over everything.

But Nina calms down and lies back, staring up at the sky. The clouds above are drifting along, swirling from dark into light. "I hope they never find you, Cameron."

I feel a tiny drop of rain on my cheek. "We're a burden, you know," I say.

We are quiet for a minute. Waves are rolling through my brain, but I don't want to tell her, because just like her, I don't want this moment to end. Nina seems to have forgotten that she's mad, and I can still taste her lips on mine. But my mind is like an ocean lapping against the shore of my skull. I wait a minute for my brain to calm down and then say, "What's your depression like, Nina?"

"Like a brick," she says. "Like a big lump of nothing sitting square in the middle of my head. Sometimes it feels like I can barely keep my head up."

"Do you think if your mom cared more, it'd be better?"

"They say it has to do with the chemistry in my brain. If that's true, how she feels wouldn't make any difference."

I want to say more, but something is plugging up my thoughts so that my words don't come out right.

"Cam?"

"Yes, babe."

"I'm sorry I got that way about your girlfriend. It just gets to me."

"It's okay," I say. But the dark swirling feeling rumbles in my brain and I tense up.

Back off, boy. Don't get too close.

"Why not?"

Because she'll control you.

"Cam? Are you okay? Are you talking to her?"

"No," I say. "But I think I need to get up."

Nina jumps up. She pulls on me and I stand on shaky legs. They seem disconnected from the rest of my body, and when I try to walk normally, one leg stretches way out in front like a cartoon clown's big foot.

"Let me," Nina says, and she grabs hold of one arm and guides me back to the carport.

It's as if I were watching myself as that cartoon clown, and each step seems more hilarious than the last. Only I'm not laughing anymore.

"I wish there was a place for me," I say as we make it to the back steps.

Nina opens the door and says, "I've got one right here."

#

Her mom's bedspread is draped over me, and it looks like some old English king's robe. Nina is in the kitchen, cutting even slices of pepperoni she brought home from the store.

The bed feels like a waterbed and I'm sloshing back and forth. But something is changing. If I close my eyes, I can see dark lines like expanding veins blaze new trails in my head. Nina comes in and gives me a handful of pepperoni. "If you finish that, you can have some Swedish Fish," she says.

She sits down carefully and I wait for the sloshing to stop. "Nina," I say.

A pepperoni stick juts out of her mouth. "What?"

"I wish I could be better for you."

She stops chewing and pulls the stick out. "Ah, Cam. How sweet."

"I just wish," I say.

She studies me for a second and then shakes her head. "I don't care," she finally says. "I don't care if you're better or not." She jams the stick back in her mouth.

Even though those veins are reproducing fast in my head, I am looking at Nina. There is a bright glow around her hair. Like one that an angel wears. "Till it's over," I say, holding up one of the pieces of pepperoni.

She nods, doing the same. "Till it's over."

twenty-one

EVEN though the screen is slightly snowy, the TV works now, and we sit in front of it waiting to see me mentioned. Only the longer I sit, the more unusual the pictures become. Nina keeps passing me chunks of pepperoni, and I take swigs of bottled tea.

I don't hear from anyone, and by late afternoon, I'm beginning to wonder if the voices are gone. I would like to feel fingers on my neck again, but all I feel is Nina touching my shoulder once in a while, and it's nice to turn and see an actual face smiling back at me.

But even Nina's smile can't take away the surreal sights I see on the TV; faces elongate and people's speech slows down and then speeds up. I fear that I cannot just will these things away, which means I'm doomed to having them for life unless I take my meds.

"No," I say out loud.

"I agree," says Nina.

Nina rubs my neck a little. I think she's getting used to me.

As it grows dark outside, Nina says, "Maybe we should have a little party." But a party is the last thing I want, and I get up and go into my bedroom. I am tired and feeling overpowered, and I didn't even get a chance to see myself on the TV screen. I plop on the bed and close my eyes. Sometime in the night, I feel the bed shake and I roll over.

#

The next morning I feel a lump of pepperoni in my gut. When I turn over, I can feel Nina next to me. I can hear her too. You never really know a person until you hear her snoring. She's talking, only not to me.

"You can't do it," she says, and she sounds like she really means it. She kicks out her leg and nearly catches my hip. I grab her leg and it feels smooth. Goose bumps rise on my arms.

`The incidence of teen pregnancy is . . .`

"Stop," I whisper to The Professor.

The incidence is zero if you don't try.

"He loves me, loves me not," says a sleeping Nina.

I'm antsy, and I pull on my pants and shirt and leave her in the bed. I look in the fridge and find some milk that Nina bought the day before. I drink half a quart from the carton and put it back in. I don't like the way I feel. Electric jolts are starting at my shoulders and zapping along my arms. I will them to stop but I have no power. I start pacing back and forth in the living room. I need to stop this from going further, but my brain is all tied up in knots, and the rumble there is not getting any softer.

"Try to get focused," Dr. Simons always says.

"Each step I take," I say in rhythm with my feet. "Each step I take brings me closer to my destination." This nonsense used to calm me. Over and over again it flies out of my mouth. "Each step. Each step. Each step." I can feel my voice rather than hear it as it rises to a crescendo. Back and forth I go. Faster and faster my voice drums out the words. "Each step."

Each step.

"Each step." Until I'm practically screaming.

"Cameron!"

Nina is in the doorway dressed in her rumpled clothes from yesterday.

"Cameron," she mouths again.

I can see the letters of my name as they float out of her mouth and travel across the room.

Catch them.

The *C* leads because it is a capital letter, and the others bunch up behind it. They float so close that I put my hand out and try to grab them. Instead, my hand chops through them, spreading them like oily swirls in the air. I watch as they regroup and form my name again before floating to my ear. Then I can hear them.

"Cameron."

Crazy fun.

Then slow, deep laughter.

Across the room, I see words pouring out of Nina's mouth again, a lot of them, but I put my hands up to protect myself and try to back up so they won't find me. I hunker down behind a chair. "Don't talk," I manage to say. "Please, don't talk. Don't talk."

Good old Nina. She eases into a chair and peeks over the top. Looking at me, she makes a zipping-her-lips motion. Then she gives me the "What is it?" look.

"Something's wrong," I say. "Way wrong."

"What?" she asks, and then clamps a hand over her mouth. But it's too late. I can see the *W* looking for me. It and the *h* manage to find my ear. The *a* and the *t* are hiding somewhere in the room.

"I'm lost," I say, but Nina shakes her head violently. She reaches over and grabs one of my arms, pulling me up. She puts a finger to her lips and then crooks it, asking me to follow her. I stumble along until we hit the bathroom. She takes my shoulders and puts me in front of the mirror hanging on the medicine cabinet.

I'm shocked. My hair is jutting out all over. My lips have a funny white gluey substance on them that keeps them closed. My eyes are sunk deep into my head, but what I can see of them is flashing a red signal light. Nina is pointing at me.

"Not lost," she squeaks out, and the letters stay put in her mouth. "Right here."

She's great, but I want to tell her it's like putting a little Band-Aid on a slashed throat.

I can feel myself rise up to the ceiling of the bathroom and then ease back down. I hear a click when I connect with the floor again.

Nina taps on my shoulder. "Cameron?"

"Whose zere?" I say.

"Are you all right? What happened?"

"A lot at the same time," I say. "A lot."

"Like what things?" I finally look her in the eye and can see fear but also genuine concern. "The voices again?"

"Something different." I point to my eyes. "Tricks on me."

"Oh, Cameron." Nina gathers me in and squeezes me tightly from the side. My chin comes to rest on top of her head. I smell her hair, a smoky spice. I hear her voice resonate through me. "I worry about you," she says.

It feels like I could drift up again, but there is a knock on the front door, and it jolts both of us. Nina looks up at me.

"It could be my mom," she says. She lets go and steps out into the hall.

"Cops?" I blubber.

"Then it had better be me who goes out to meet them," she says.

She disappears and I wait. I open the medicine cabinet and see bottles of pills lined up on all the shelves. I slam it shut when she comes back.

"It's some guy and your sister," she says.

"Beffy?"

"It's the girl you wave to on the bus."

Nina drags me out to a place by the front door where we can peek without being seen. I move the curtain slightly and see Beth and Dylan waiting patiently.

"What do we do?" asks Nina.

I don't answer. Instead, I turn the deadbolt and open the door. Beth's eyes open wide when she sees me. She grabs Dylan's hand and pulls him inside with her.

"Jesus," she says as she hugs me. "You look dead or something."

"Heigh-ho, Beffy," I say.

Beth takes my chin and forces me to look in her eyes. "You're not okay," she pronounces.

"You look like shit," Dylan says.

"But how did you know where he was?" Nina asks.

Beth turns and finally looks at her. "Are you that girl?" she says.

"Nina," Nina says.

Beth turns back to me. "It's not important how I found you. Jesus, Cam, they're dredging the river for you."

"You're on the news big-time," Dylan says. "The police, the sheriff's department, everybody is looking for you. They're even talking about a reward."

"Go get that bag in the car," Beth tells him, and he immediately obeys, pulling the door closed a little too hard. "I'm worried," she says to me.

I want to tell her to save me, but I can't get the words out. I snatch a look at Nina, and she raises an eyebrow.

"Are they looking for me, too?" she says.

"They don't mention you," Beth says. "I don't know what the deal is, Cam, but sooner or later they're going to find you, and then there'll be worse trouble. I don't think you want that."

"New life," I say. But I lose the rest of my thought, and luckily Dylan comes bustling through the door, carrying Beth's old suitcase. He sets it on the floor.

"I brought you some things," Beth says. "I thought you might be a little grungy by now. Plus, there are some chips and stuff to eat."

"Goody goofy," I say.

She pulls me aside and talks in a whisper. "Mom's a wreck, just so you know. She's crying all the time. Dad's got that look; you know, his mouth is a straight line. They're hurting badly, Cam. And it looks like you are too."

It's as if I can feel the hurt as a knife slicing into my belly. I put my hand there.

"Come home," Beth says.

"Home, home on the range," I say.

Beth looks like she's struggling with that. She reaches up and kisses me on the forehead. "Come back home," she says. "I promise it'll be better."

Dylan points a pistol finger at me and winks as they

go out the door. Both Nina and I look out the window as they get in the car and drive away. I see Beth staring back at the house until they're out of sight.

I feel numb and it looks like Nina does too. She goes over and sits down, fingers at her lips.

"Gonna be okay," I say.

But she shakes her head. "I just wonder why nobody ever knows my name. I'm always just 'that girl.'"

"Know your name," I say, pointing to myself.

But Nina's not buying it. "Don't you ever mention me to anybody?" she asks.

I'm not sure what to say, and the look on her face tells me it's a more important question than it seems. "Don't tell them any friends' names," I say.

"How many friends do you have besides Griffin?" she says. She gets up and walks past me and into her bedroom. I've seen it on TV before; I should follow her in and try to make up, but I can't get my feet to move.

Instead, I go back to the door and pick up the suitcase. I lug it over to the chair and sit down. I unzip it and dig through T-shirts, undies, a bag of cookies, some chips, a deck of cards. And at the bottom, a photo of the four of us: Mom, Dad, Beth, and I at the beach. I'm five years old. My hair is flapping in the wind, and I have a big smile on my face. We all do.

I put the picture on the end table and stare at it. In

the background I hear the ticking of the clock, but time doesn't matter to me now. I feel myself pulled toward the picture, and then I'm sucked into it.

Now my family is beside me, but I can't touch them, can't get their attention. All they do is stare out into the room. Hours seem to pass as I stand like a statue in the picture with my family. I think and it makes no difference. I wonder about life and I don't move a muscle. It could be days and days and everything would still be the same. Never a change. Never.

All my systems are blocked up. Almost all. One thing starts to pound at my brain, and I can't get it to go away.

Not right to hurt, I think.

But you want to be cool, don't you? You want to be the man?

It is twilight now, and if I don't do something, I could be stuck in the picture forever. When I finally manage to slip out of it, my mouth works again. "I don't know," I say.

Sure you do. Every guy does. For once in your life be the guy people remember.

"Not for that," I say.

Go for it.

I grit my teeth and slap my face, then slap it again. I whisper, "The Girl, The Girl, The Girl. Please help."

No answer.

Attaboy. Keep hitting yourself. Get yourself all worked up first.

`Chopped liver here. This is not the direction you want to go in.`

Do it.

"Do what?"

What do you think I've been saying? Haven't you been listening?

And then I do know what he's talking about. I feel pleasure at the same time that I feel pain. And there's nothing I can do about it. Like some weird android, I stand up and walk toward Nina's bedroom.

"Somebody stop me," I say.

Attaboy. Good boy. Man, is this going to be good.

"No good."

You know it's good.

"Not what I want. Not me."

You know where she is. This will be what finally makes you the man.

"The Girl?" I say.

Keep going.

"Please. Got to stop." But I am under this voice's control. I can't stop my feet from moving. I'm in the kitchen. It is quiet and dark everywhere, except in my head.

Right turn.

"Not me." But I turn right.

There she is. See her there, crying her little eyes out. She's waiting for you, big guy. She wants you so badly.

A low lamp is lighted on her bedside table, and I can see Nina face-down on the bed. I make her suffer and suffer and I don't even know why. My throat catches.

Doesn't it make you feel, you know, a little tight?

"I don't like this."

You will. Then you'll be a man.

I stand in her doorway and look at her. Even through the gauze of crazy I can see there's something not quite right with her.

Touch her.

I whisper again. "Please help."

And it finally comes.

Am I some genie you can conjure up when you need me?

"I do need you."

I can see that.

"Can't you help me?"

If you do it, it would be like doing it with me.

"What? No, help me."

Do now what you need to do, and then I'll help you.

"What I need to do?" I look at Nina on the bed. This doesn't sound like The Girl.

I love you, Cameron.

The Professor's voice, but The Girl's words.

Do it. Now The Girl's voice.

I love you, *but you must do it;* **remember the old nobody Cameron?** Is that what you want to be again?

I raise my hands high in the air. Everything's all mixed up. "Stop talking!" I shout in a voice the neighbors should have been able to hear. Only Nina seems not to.

Do it now. Touch her, touch her, touch her.

I take a step into the room and see the bottle on the bed. A couple of pills have fallen out of it, and it is now empty. It takes all my self-control to bend down and look at Nina. Her breath is ragged, her face a pasty white.

This is where you dig deep, Cameron Galloway.

"Oh God," I hear. "Help her."

And it's my very own voice this time.

twenty-two

NOW the only thing I know how to do well is run. So I sprint out of the room, out of the house, and to the middle of the street.

Get help.

No. Just do it.

"Help!" I call as I turn in a circle. "Help me! Help her!"

My words are gibberish. "Girl! Pills! Dying! Help! Girl. Pills. Dying. Help." Over and over I say it until a guy comes out of his house with a cell phone at his ear. Seeing him, I run back into Nina's house.

Minutes later, I'm clown-walking in the front room when they break through the door and come in with their trunks and their bags and their gurney. I try to go back with them, but one guy shoves me out of the way, and I retreat to the living room.

You could sneak out. Find a new home.

"Leave me alone."

Do you think I'm just some girl you can boss around? Some professor? Who do you think's in charge?

It's been only a few minutes, and they're out with Nina on a stretcher. She already has a tube hooked up to her arm, and her face is just as washed out as it was when I found her. I back up, step by step, and run into a pair of feet. I turn, and there stands a policeman.

"I guess you'd be Cameron Galloway," he says.

"Might be."

He takes me by the arm and I don't resist. "There are a lot of folks waiting to see you," he says.

I try to pull away, but he holds me fast. "I'm fourteen," I say. "Can make my own mind up."

"Is that so?" says the cop. "Well, I'm thirty-eight and I can too. My decision is to take you into custody as a material witness."

"No." I want to fight, but I don't have it in me. And when I realize this, a strange thing happens. I give in, and the whole house lights up like a rainbow strobe. The cop's head is pulsating with light. It runs along his arm and jumps onto me. I can feel the current follow my nerve paths.

"Come on, then," he says, and we step out just in time to see the ambulance take Nina away.

People have gathered in the neighborhood, and up above them floats a cloud of letters bumping into each other. It's what you call a hubbub. I let the cop take me to his prowler and put me in the back seat. It's quieter there. I can see the cop through the screen separating the two of us. He's on his radio, telling them he found me.

I'm scared, Cameron. What's going on?

"Arrested," I say.

"No, not arrested," the cop says as he places his radio back in its home. "Just held."

He's scary.

"You bother my girlfriend," I say.

The cop takes a peek back at me, rolls his eyes, and then starts up his car. We back out of the driveway, and a group of people parts to let us through.

The cop is back on the radio again, but all I pick up is the word *hospital.*

Don't let them split us up, Cam. We're all we've got. If they split us, we can't make it.

"Do what I can do."

I love you, Cam.

I lean my head against the window. My energy is leaking out of my shoes, and I feel more and more like a husk. "Where are you going?" I ask.

"To your folks. Don't you think they've suffered enough?"

I don't want to go home, but there's not much I can do locked in the back of a cop's car.

Use your sneaky brain.

I try the only thing that comes to my failing mind. I start batting at my legs. "Off! Off! Eating me alive!" I throw myself from one side of the back seat to the other. "Help me!" I squeal. Ten more seconds of this and the cop's back on the radio, and instead of driving to my house, he takes a sharp right turn toward Saint John's.

#

At Saint John's, they are already working on Nina when the cop brings me in. As soon as I get inside, I stop the screaming and just look around with my eyes open wide. A nurse takes me to a special room, tells me my parents are on their way, and rubs my arm for a few minutes while she talks about how drugs are taking over our youth.

I try to ignore her, but it is a small room. "Smell you," I say.

She jerks back and narrows her eyes.

"Smells like bad medicine."

After a moment, her pager goes off and she stands up and says, "I'm going to trust you to stay here till the doctor comes."

"All right," I say.

Get ready.

As soon as she's gone, I'm out of the room. She's walking right, so I sneak down the wall to the left. I pass a couple of examining rooms and then round the corner to the real emergencies. Most of the curtains are drawn in a funny crescent, but the one in the middle of the room is closed, and I can see feet everywhere on the inside.

"Lavage!" someone barks as I step closer. I can see people working through the curtain. Nina is stretched out on a bed with a tube already down her throat.

"We'll lose her if you don't start that lavage, stat!"

The voice is growly and primal, and it's hard to tell where it's coming from. I jump back from the curtain. My stomach feels knotted up. I don't want to hear this. I don't want to know what's going to happen. But when I start toward the other side of the room, my nurse spies me and says, "Hey!"

I spin and take off the other way. Over my shoulder, I hear her shout, "I need Security!"

My shoes start acting as if they're packed with

concrete. My knees feel weaker. I duck into one of the examining rooms and wait. Outside the door, I hear my nurse and some guy.

"He went running," she says. "He probably took off outside."

Then I hear footsteps recede down the hall. I take a deep breath and carefully turn the knob. All clear one way and all clear the other. I want to run in my concrete feet, but I'm not sure which way to go. The dilemma is solved when my nurse turns the corner again and sees me. Before she can get a word out, I spin around and take off in the other direction. I'm tracing the way I came in and hope the cop isn't still lurking around when I get to the lobby. Lucky me. The way is clear to the front door and I bust through it running.

I manage to find a good hiding spot in a stand of scrub fir. I watch the Security guy do a cursory look around the grounds and then go back inside. I sit and wait. It did not seem good for Nina back in the ER, but if I were to go in again, they'd nab me and I might never find out what happened to her.

It is just a few minutes later when I think I'm hearing yet another voice. But it turns out to be a familiar one. "It's time for new rules," my dad says, and I turn toward the sound.

My family is piling out of our car: Dad, Mom, Beth,

and even Dylan. I clench my fists. Beth has never been a snitch before. I watch them hurry across the parking lot, wondering what is going on in their heads. Even from a distance I can tell my mom's eyes are bright red. My dad's face has new worry lines. When Dylan slips through the ER door, I stand up. I look at the car.

You know you can.

"Know it," I say.

Then why not?

"Don't know if I can drive."

Anybody can drive.

I walk over to the car and stand, listening to the ticking of the engine as it cools.

You know where it is.

And I do. I reach to the space below one of the wipers and find the magnetic box my dad uses to hide the spare key. I rattle it.

It's a good sound, buddy boy. You know what it's the sound of?

"Freedom," I whisper.

You got that right.

Again, Cameron, we've reached a point where you can do the right thing. The chances of a fourteen-year-old boy coming to some bad end driving a car he has never learned to drive are well over 80 percent.

Now, where do you get those phony numbers?

Hello, Cam. Hello, hello, hello. I would look good snuggled up next to you in this car.

That clinches it. Despite my footloose brain, I unlock the door and slide into the driver's seat. It smells of my family and makes me feel a little more in control again. No wonder my dad likes to be here. I plug the key into the ignition and switch it on.

It roars and I like it. I keep pushing down the pedal and letting this beast get it all out. A couple walking by raise their eyebrows at me, so I give it a little more gas just to make my point. My foot feels funny, and I look down to see that somewhere along the way I've lost a shoe. But I don't have time to look for it and instead put my hand on the gearshift.

Here we go.

I pull the shift back to reverse and give it a little too much gas. I shoot out into the lot and practically squeal the tires when I slam on the brakes. The car bounces and then settles.

I put it in D and gently move ahead, going around the circle to the exit. Too late, I realize this is a pay lot. I ease up to the window and search in the ashtray where Dad keeps his change. There I find the slip. I pass it to the guy at the window.

"One dollar," he says tiredly, holding out his hand.

I yank out four quarters and give them to him. He doesn't even look at me as I take off and nearly clip a car when I pull into the street. Driving is all new to me, but it's not as hard as they make you think it is. Pretty soon, I know I can do it.

Next problem. Where am I supposed to go? I know I haven't got much time. My parents will look for me at the hospital, but then they'll come out and see that their car is missing. After that, every cop in town will be looking out for my license plate.

So I head to the one place I figure they wouldn't think to look for me. Home.

Home? Blah.

It's where the heart is. Good idea, young man.

I get on the West Side Highway and pick up speed. I'm weaving a little and tapping the brake too much, but after a while, it's easy to keep the car on my side of the white line. Pretty soon, I'm passing under the railroad bridge, and I freeze when I think of how just a while ago I was up there risking my life. I can do this.

My parents must have been in a hurry, because the back door is standing open. I sneak into the kitchen and listen. No sounds except for the gentle sigh of the furnace. In the refrigerator I find leftovers; roast beef slices under plastic wrap, macaroni and cheese in a casserole dish. I pull both of them out and head for the microwave.

Oh good, I'm starved.

Me too.

When the microwave buzzes, I take the food to the table. Without thinking, I pull out my dad's chair and sit down. I stuff a piece of beef in my mouth but stop when I look down the length of our table. One chair on each side, and one on each end. It seems a long way down there now.

It's as if you're the dad and I'm the mom.

And I'm the bad son.

Great, I'd like to introduce myself to everyone. You can call me chopped liver.

Something gnaws at my stomach as I get up and pull down two plates from the cupboard. I put one in front of me and one at my right side. I scoop out some mac and cheese and spoon it onto the other plate.

"There you go," I say.

You've beaten the odds, and they were pretty stiff odds. Sadly, the odds of getting out of this particular situation are zero. Please, Cameron, let's think about this.

I get up and retrieve yet another plate from the cupboard. I lay a piece of beef on this one and shove the plate to my left. "Don't you want me to be happy?" I ask The Professor.

This is what you call happiness?

You've still got work to do, bud.

"Work?"

The best you can be. Remember? Before we're through, you'll be driving all the way to Mexico.

Instinctively, I take another plate out. On this one, I put on a little of each. I take aim and push it down the length of the table like a shuffleboard game. It stops a foot from the end.

My hands shake. There's a pounding in my head. The voices keep screaming and I can't get a word in. And I don't know who's on my side.

twenty-three

I HAVE opened the floodgates.

You were just going to make life better for her.

That's rude and you know it. Cam, who is this guy? Isn't that rude? You'd never be cruel to her. She's a friend of ours.

Oh, what's a friend, anyway? Do it with her and then move on. Who cares whether she wants to or not? That's what I say. Then your troubles are over and your new life can start. You, of all people, would like that.

What is that supposed to mean?

"Enough," I say. But this doesn't work. And I feel my mind start to break, the pieces, like drifting ice floes, occupied by these voices. I put my hands on my head and try to squeeze the pieces back together. And then it is absolutely quiet. Even the ticking of the furnace has stopped. Just like in Nina's bathroom, I feel myself rise from the table and clutch desperately at its edge to hang on.

"What's happening?"

I rise but the chair moves with me. I lift above the chattering voices. I climb higher and higher to where they sound like little mouse voices, like the little rabbit girl at school. I have risen above them, but in actuality I haven't moved at all. I close my eyes and start spinning, like a diver who has leaped from the board and tucked his knees into his chest. Faster and faster I go until I believe that I can spin right out of my life into some great void where people like me spend eternity just spinning. I spin so fast that the voices resemble different strings of color in a blender.

And now I can see without opening my eyes. I can see through my eyelids, and I see them all. I see The Professor with his carefully shaved goatee. I see The Other Guy with his torn T-shirt and baggy pants and the way he slouches in the chair. His voice disengages from the blend and says:

I'll take you where you want to go.

"Go away," I say. But I sense a weakness in my voice.

And then I see The Girl. I see her so clearly that it makes me suck in a big breath. I've been waiting and waiting, and here finally is the love of my life. I want to drink in what I see. I want to reach out and feel her tender milky skin. She's everything I dreamed of: the lips, the eyes, the body all rolled into one beautiful girl. And there's so much I want to say. I want to quote all the poets I've ever heard of, all of Shakespeare's sonnets, but all that comes out is, "I wish, I wish."

Then I hear another voice, a new one at the table.

"Cameron?"

Against my will, I finally stretch out of my spin. My body lengthens and I point my hands straight ahead of me. Soon, I will cut into the water in a perfect dive. But before that happens, I open my eyes to find myself still sitting at the table. All around me are the plates humped with food. Something taps me on the shoulder. I turn to see my father standing there.

"Cameron?" he says. "Settle down, son." He pats me and it feels like a cool rag on my forehead.

"Pop," I say.

He holds my shoulder tighter. "We've been looking all over for you. Your mom has been scared out of her wits."

I look around for her and he reads my mind.

"They're all at the hospital, hoping you'll come back. I was sent out to see if I could find you. Only I couldn't even find our car in the parking lot. Where it was supposed to be, I found this." He holds up one of my shoes. I look down and see its match on one foot.

I cough and my throat feels raspy. "Nina?" I ask.

"I don't know," he says as he hands me the shoe, and when I get it on, he starts steering me toward the door. "Is there anything you want from here?"

"Peace," I say.

We ride the way we usually ride — not much is said. I'm easily distracted, and I can feel my head shooting side to side, back and forth. Dad is humming, but not loud enough for me to recognize the song. He's in his work clothes, and there's a crease down his pant leg. When we get to the railroad bridge, I point to it and say, "Climbed that once."

"Did you, now?" he says. "That's a ways up."

"Yeah, the wind was blowing hard and the rails were slick—"

"Cam," he says. "That's enough now."

He might as well have stuck me with a knife. He checks his rearview mirror and speeds up. He looks scared. The strongest people in the world can still be afraid.

I feel myself being pushed aside. Soon, I can't tell what is real. Am I really traveling down the West Side Highway with my dad, or am I just making it up, or is somebody making it up for me?

It doesn't matter. Life is all made up.

"No," I say.

My dad sneaks a peek from the corner of his eye.

"I mean yes," I add.

What if my dad isn't real? What if all of life isn't even real and your real life takes place on some alternate planet? Where only voices live? I think of what The Girl said. What if we are the voices in *their* heads?

"That would suck," I say out loud.

We get to the hospital, and my dad parks almost exactly in the same spot as before. He holds on to me extra tight as we walk toward the ER. Instead of glass, the door looks like a solid dark entrance, covering up something evil that's going to happen inside.

"Oh my God," my mom shouts as she sees us come through. She runs up and pulls my head into her. I can hear her sniffling in my ear. "I thought you were dead."

"I should be," I say. And I can feel her pull back just the tiniest bit.

"Don't say that," she says into my shoulder.

I know times like this are supposed to feel comforting, but the truth is, I still can't feel anything right now. My emotional pump, the machine that dredges up the right way to feel, has completely broken down.

Beth and Dylan are standing back near the nurse's station. Beth has her hand in Dylan's. She smiles at me, but I close my eyes.

Just reach right up and put your hands around her throat. Then they'll know you mean business.

"No," I say loudly, and I pull back from my mom. "Not what I want." She tries to get ahold of me, but I slap her hand away.

"Cameron," she barks. "Stop that."

My dad's big hand comes out and clamps on my shoulder like a vise. "That will be the end of that, young man."

"I've got to find Nina," I say.

"Then we will go with you," Dad says.

He steers me with his tight grip. Dylan and Beth part to let me pass.

I whisper "Benedict Armpit" as I slip through them. I am determined to find Nina. That is, until I turn the corner and there stands Dr. Simons, wearing a white coat and holding the end of the world in his hand.

"You told me," I say. "You said I could make up my own mind."

"Cameron," he says as he steps toward me, carrying the syringe. "I said that's true as long as you can take care of yourself. If you can't take care of yourself, then the law provides for the state to take over."

I step back and run into my father. I can feel the heat from his body. "This is a free country," I say. I expect my dad's hands to hold me again, but instead Dr. Simons holds up the syringe.

"You need rest," the doctor says.

"No, wait. Not yet. Where's Nina? Got to talk to her first."

"Cam." It's my mother lurking behind my father.

"Don't talk to me," I say.

"It's best if you come along," says Dr. Simons.

I look at him and then to my family. I see fear in everybody's eyes, but it's not the kind of fear that makes them run the other way. It's more the kind that's worried about what I might do to myself. It makes my dreams sag.

"Okay," I say to Dr. Simons. "But they have to stay out."

I know I've hurt them, but this is too important for me to have them looking over my shoulder. Dr. Simons takes me by the arm, and we walk down the hall. About halfway down, he motions me to a room.

The lights are bright and twinkling off shiny yellow walls, and I have to shade my eyes till I get used to them. Dr. Simons motions for me to get up on the examining table. The paper crackles as I do.

"I don't want to do this," I complain.

"I know," he says. He starts rolling up my sleeve, but I pull it away.

"No, I really don't want it to be over."

"What don't you want to be over?"

I look back on the last few weeks and think about what I've done. "My good life."

Your good life? You mean the best life ever. It doesn't have to go away, and you know it.

Dr. Simons nods and looks down at the syringe before catching my eye. "From my point of view, your face doesn't look all that good. Actually, you look scared."

"But that's good," I plead. "At least I feel something."

Although I do feel afraid of the voice that keeps getting stronger and meaner, I also know Dr. Simons knows absolutely nothing about living with fear and how much better it is than living with nothing. But I've never gone this far before, and I just don't know for sure.

"I want to ask you one question first," I say. "You never did answer it before."

"All right."

"Is it possible to keep only some of the voices, or do I have to keep them all?"

Keep them all, big boy. You can handle them all.

Dr. Simons sets down the syringe and pets his chin with his fingers. "I can't exactly say for sure, but my guess would be that you can't pick and choose. You get what you're given."

Pick it up. Pick up the needle and . . .

I want to trust Dr. Simons, and it feels like he's talking from the heart. "But that's not fair," I say. "With everything wrong with me, can't I have just this one thing?"

"You're right, Cameron. It's not fair."

It's as if I've exhausted all my options. No pardons for the crazy boy. "Can I have a few minutes by myself?"

He is skeptical and I don't blame him.

"I won't do anything," I say. "I promise."

He nods. "But this time there'll be someone right outside the door." He picks up the syringe as he leaves.

#

He's gone and I can breathe easier. Around me I see jars filled with absorbent swabs and tongue depressors. The walls tell stories about how to prevent the flu. My body feels jittery, as if I've had too much caffeine for three weeks. I kick at the base of the table. I am a hostage here. The rest of the world is outside the door. The rest of my life lives in that syringe Dr. Simons is guarding.

Hello, Cam. That was a close one. There must be some way out of this.

"God, I've been waiting forever to really talk to you."

What's the plan, Cam? Is it a good one like the railroad bridge?

"We have to talk," I say.

My favorite thing.

"I don't think I have a plan," I say.

There is a silence like death. Now it seems as if the whole world has its ear pressed against the door.

Are you just going to let them do this to us?

"No. Course not," I quickly say, but then, more slowly, "but I don't know what to do."

So you're giving in? Listen to me—it doesn't have to be this way.

"It's all changed."

What's changed?

"The Other Guy. I saw him at the table. I don't know what to do with him, and he's getting worse. It's as if he's taking control. Can't you feel him?"

He's not that bad.

"He almost made me hurt Nina."

Oh, her.

"Nina's a good person. I don't want to hurt her."

But you want to hurt me, Cam.

I take a moment to collect my thoughts. They are a jumble still, and I have to pick and choose the words that float by. "But Nina's real," I finally say.

And me?

I hear sniffles.

"You? You're perfect."

Perfect isn't enough for you?

"I don't know," I say. "All I know is that I don't want to hurt anybody." I struggle for the words. "But it's too hard to be normal right now." When I say this, a strange feeling occupies my mind, as if I were shaking, but my hands are calm. "Are you okay?"

I've just heard I'm not good enough. And I'm about to go away forever. Would you be okay if that happened to you?

I can't talk because of the big rock in my throat.

I'm sorry. I didn't mean to hurt you. I was just being, you know, me.

"I love you," I finally say. "I've never known anyone like you before."

Oh, Cam. We've been through so much together. Remember the bridge?

"Yes."

And the roof? Sleeping in the same bed?

"I do remember."

And telling off Mrs. Owens the way we did?

Laughter.

Can't I please stay?

So this is what it's like to feel real pain. My heart is wrenched and I grab at my chest. Is this normal? Is this what I want in my life? "I can't," I say. "I wish I could keep you, but I can't. That other guy, he's taking over."

Oh, Cam. Sometimes you have to take the bad with the good.

From out of nowhere, I see a little peephole of light deep in my brain. "They tell me you're just a voice I hear in my head," I say.

I hear her sweet laughter again.

That's so funny, isn't it? I mean, when you and I both know different.

"We do?"

You and I both know that you're a voice in my *head.*

I still can't take this in. My mind flails from one idea to another.

You make me stronger, Cam. I can't live this life without you.

"But, no. It's not . . ." But she may be right. Who am I to say? Maybe I had it entirely backwards all along. Maybe I was right before about my dad and the whole family, my whole life, not being real. I shake my head. Does this guessing never stop?

Cameron. I don't want us to die. Please.

One recognizes the finality of this moment. One has chosen well. We all must find our own places.

"But it still hurts," I say.

I hear The Girl's sadness and feel like I've betrayed my best friend. Feel my own failure. I realize it's now or never. If I don't do something now, I may never get out alive.

I step down from the table and open the door. True to his word, Dr. Simons is standing right outside it. The rest of my family is grouped not far away. I guess they won't make the same mistake twice at this hospital. Dr. Simons comes in and takes the cap off the syringe.

"You ready?" he says.

I nod and close my eyes, thinking about love and understanding and the ups and downs of my life. Then I feel a touch on the back of my neck, and fingers caress me. Her fingers. I reach out and grab Dr. Simons's arm and hold tightly. There is a slight pinprick, and then I feel a thick solution infiltrating the muscle in my arm. But unlike in the past, I'm calmer now as it works its way inside me.

"I love you," I say, but I hear nothing back.

epilogue

THEY have me on the fifth floor at Saint John's again. It's the loony bin, but they call it Five West. That's so it won't hurt our feelings. And believe me, they're all about feelings here. I share a room with two other guys, but they're way out of it, so we don't talk much.

They tell me it's three days later and that I've been sedated most of that time. I feel logy, but I'm mostly awake and I can follow what's going on on the TV overhead. My brain is back to the way it's felt for most of the time since all this started. Cobwebby. There is a tiny militiaman at every neuron, making sure nothing and nobody gets through. Since we are supposedly the type that can never control our feelings, they make sure no big unmanageable ones ever crop up.

I'm up now, wearing a stupid gown. At least they let me put on my boxers underneath. I look in the mirror and see a stranger. My hair is stiff and stands straight up like shaved wheat. My teeth are protected by a thick coat of ugly film. It is in this fine state that I greet Dr. Simons.

He's as cheerful as ever. "Okay, then," he says. "I see the patient has swum up to consciousness." His white coat flows around him like swirling snow as he hurries into the room. "You feeling okay?"

I shrug. "How am I supposed to feel?"

"Good, good," he says. "Listen, I think we'll be letting you go home in a couple of days. How's that sound?"

I twirl my finger in the air.

"Good, good. Well, we can talk about all this later. For now, you're making a good recovery, and that's what we're most concerned about. Anything else?"

"I was wondering if you could tell me about Nina."

"Ah yes, Nina," he says, his eyebrows curving down. But then they do an immediate uplift. "You know about confidentiality, Cameron."

One of those little brain guards must have been asleep on the job because upon hearing this, I feel a rush of pleasure. "She's alive, then?"

"I can neither confirm nor deny that."

We both know what he's really saying. "Thank you," I say.

"A little later, your parents are coming," he says. "I want us all to talk."

"Okay."

"In case you wanted to go for a little walk on the ward," he says, "room five-oh-eight has some interesting elements to it."

When he's gone, I reach under the bed with one foot and pull out my slippers. Snuggling into them, I venture out into the hall. There is a quiet hum all around. It's not like a regular floor; here people don't need clanging surprises. I immediately walk down and check out the numbers on the doors: 511, 510, 509. I stop in front of 508. The door is slightly ajar, and I can see shadows moving around inside. I'm about to knock, but the door swings open and a young woman in a pale blue uniform comes out carrying plastic trays. She sets them on a cart near the door.

"Is it okay to go inside?" I ask.

"Sure," she says. "She's awake and she's the only one in there."

Nina's sitting up against the pillows, brushing her hair, and the first thing I notice is how pink her face is compared with when I last saw her.

"I was wondering when you would stop by."

"I'm here too," I say.

"Yeah, I can see that." She sets down the brush, and some of the thin strands of her hair try to go with it.

"I'm sorry," I say.

"For what? You didn't do anything."

"But I should have—"

"Listen, Cam, it's demeaning to try to convince me I can't make up my own mind. It was my idea to do what I did. Not yours."

This is not going the way I thought it might, so I find a chair and sit down at the side of her bed.

"I'm back on the meds," I say.

"Yeah." She licks at her lips and adds, "So am I. So much for going our own way."

"I'm sorry," I say. "I wish you didn't take so many."

She starts brushing her hair again.

"I saw all my voices at the table in my house," I say.

She turns to look out the window. "I don't think I want to share war stories about your psychosis."

"I'm just saying." I start to feel shaky, so I stand up.

She runs the brush once more through her hair. "Well, I guess I'll see you," I say.

"Did the doc give you a discharge date?"

"A couple of days. How about you?"

She shrugs. "He hasn't said. He wants me to go to these gross-out groups, but I don't think I will."

"Yeah. Well, hold out for what you think is right." I raise my fist and shake it.

"Cameron, I need to tell you something," she says. She takes in a deep breath. "The time with you, even when it got a little crazy, was the best I've ever had."

"But look what you did to yourself," I remind her.

"So you can imagine what the rest of my life's been like." She bites her lip.

I've got to learn this from Nina, this knack of taking life for what it is. "Can I come back and visit while we're both still here?" I ask.

A trace of a smile plays on her lips. "Sure," she says. "And we can lock the door and let them try to break us up." Then she turns away and stares out the window again. But before I'm out the door, I hear her say, "I want you to practice this. It's *N-i-n-a*. Nina. That's my name. Remember it."

#

True to his word, Dr. Simons has the family all grouped together later that afternoon. Even Beth is there, but she looks nervous to be on this particular floor.

"Well, I think we can all breathe a sigh of relief," Dr. Simons says. "We've dodged a bullet this time."

"Can we please not use gun metaphors?" says my mom.

"Sorry," Dr. Simons says. "First off, do you have any questions?"

He's looking at me, but it's my dad who answers. "We'd like to know what the future holds."

"Excellent question," Dr. Simons says, rubbing his hands together. "And I wish I had an excellent answer. The truth is, with the kind of disease Cameron has, it's possible that he will continue to have short-term episodes for an indefinite period of time. But it's also possible that at a certain age, he could stop having episodes."

"Isn't that good news?" my mom says to me.

I shrug. It's about the hundredth time I've heard this, and I'm not as happy as my mom seems to be.

"I'm stressing the word *possible*," Dr. Simons says.

But I don't hear anything else. Dr. Simons once told me that I need to learn the difference between a vision and a fantasy, and while sitting there, I wonder if Dr. Simons needs to learn the same thing.

#

In two days I'm back home. There's no good answer to how I'm feeling. It all looks pretty much the same. In the car, I thought they might have put up ribbons or a WELCOME HOME, CAMERON sign, but it was a no-go on that one.

I sit down on my bed and dangle my hands between my legs. It's weird and doesn't make much sense. Do you put an alcoholic right back in the bar? Do you put a drug addict back out on the street? Do you put a crazy kid back in the same old house?

I hear two sets of footsteps climbing the stairs, and I quickly check to make sure I'm presentable. Mom and Dad are at the door. Dad is so tall that I can't see his hair. Mom comes to his shoulder. Both of them have that look on their face.

"Nothing," I say. "You guys did nothing wrong."

"Oh, Cam," my mom says, and she starts to break loose from Dad and rush over to me, but he holds on tight. "I don't think anybody did anything wrong."

She looks like she's ready to yak about it till morning,

so I throw up the stop sign that is my hand. "Mom, Dad. Please. I don't want to talk about it anymore."

"But Cam."

"No, I mean it. I'm just who I am. What happens to me is just me."

"But sweetie, you have to take the meds."

"I'll take the damn meds," I say. "But all the rest is just a waste of time. I don't want to waste my time anymore."

"Good boy," Dad says.

I look at him. I'll bet semipro football was a lot easier than facing a son like me. "I just don't want to be the lost kid in the family anymore. I'm tired of it. Can't I just be Cameron? I'll do what I have to do, but I want you guys to leave me alone."

"But Cam," my mom says carefully.

"I know," I say. "Can I be trusted?"

"Well?" she says.

"Probably not," I say.

My mom sighs deeply and rests her head against my dad again. "I wish you could be."

"Mom," I complain. "Come on. It was a joke."

"Is this funny?"

I have to think for a moment. "It may not be so funny, but how ridiculous is it that I, Cameron Galloway, a generally nice guy, gets stuck with a disease like this?"

"That's a mouthful," Dad says.

"I'll just have to be more vigilant," Mom says. "I'll need to check on you more and—"

I snap and say, "I guess you'll do what you have to do. But for now, I know what I have to do. In two weeks I'll be fifteen. You have no idea what I've done or what I've seen. If you did, well, you'd probably freak out or something. But I have a life. Do you hear that? I have a life and that's the way it's got to be." Out in the hall, I hear Beth snicker.

I can see that both Mom and Dad are just dying to say something, but they know better. Mom finally comes over and kisses the top of my head. Dad gives me a little nod and they're gone.

Just before their feet hit the last stair, Beth cracks open the door. "It's okay," I say. "It's all clear."

Beth has her head down as if she felt guilty about something. "I just have to say one thing," she says.

"I already know," I say. "And I forgive you for turning me in."

"Not that," she says. "I just wanted to say that when I saw the look on your face when you walked by me at the hospital, I kind of liked it."

"You did?"

"Yeah, it was like no Cameron I'd ever seen before. You looked like you knew what you were doing."

"I was completely nuts, Beth."

"Still, though."

I look up at her and smile. "Bethie, be careful. This could be catching."

"There. That's what I'm talking about. You're different. That's what I mean."

When she's gone, I get under the covers with my clothes on. Now if my parents came into my room, they'd think I was losing it again. How many guys my age accidentally fall asleep with all their clothes on? Plenty. But people don't chase those guys around with a needle filled with happy juice. The problem is, once people think a certain way about you, it's hard to get it out of their heads. It's hard to ever just be a regular guy. Everybody will always be waiting for something bad to happen. I wish it were different, but it's not.

But I think I know now what a real life is about. You can't almost get run over by a log train and not get a glimpse into something wild and imaginative. My disease may come back once in a while, but now I know I can do things I never thought I could do before, and that makes me happy. So happy, in fact, that I ease myself out of bed, grab something from my bedside table, and go to the door of my room. Opening it, I stick out my ears to see if they can pick up any noises. It sounds like the coast is clear.

It's part of my plan. It may not make sense, but I have to do this. I tiptoe down to the bathroom and lock myself in. I snap on the buzzing fluorescent light and shake a pill into my hand. I stare at it, all proud and victorious. I pick it up and flush the toilet. I can imagine the pill getting scared, latching on to my finger, and calling for help. I smile. It needs to know who the boss is. I hold it out over the swirling water and make my decision. It's one I'm going to make every day. Before the water stops gurgling, I place the pill on my tongue and swallow it. My brain needs it right now to function.

But sometimes it helps me to make my family wonder just a little.

afterword

THE disease that Cameron has is a real disease called schizophreniform disorder. It is one of the subgroups of schizophrenia, a serious affliction of the mind. What sets schizophreniform disorder apart from other schizophrenic diagnoses is that the duration and intensity of the episodes can be less severe. While schizophrenia is seen as a disease with a generally chronic course, those afflicted with schizophreniform disorder can sometimes be disease-free for significant periods of time and in some cases for the rest of their lives.

Cameron hallucinated by hearing voices, but other sufferers can have both visual and auditory hallucinations, as well as delusions. A few have even reported tactile hallucinations, like the ones Cameron experienced with The Girl. It is possible to have symptoms of this disease as early as age five. And yes, there are documented cases where individuals have carried on conversations, unafraid, with the voices in their heads.

Of all the schizophrenic diagnoses, schizophreniform disorder has the most hopeful prognosis, especially with a case like Cameron's where the sufferer functions well when he is not afflicted with symptoms. Normally, a patient like Cameron would be put on a medication regimen for one year, and then he might be slowly weaned from the medicine to see if he can function, symptom-free, without it. And so, one day Cameron might very well be free of the disease forever, which is his fondest hope.